"Kristy Noel Gillinder d
book! God has certainly gifte
with eloquence and heartfelt
she has a great story to tell. She writes with sincerity of heart and out of her own experiences where pain from life circumstances intersects with hope that can only be found in Jesus! A great and compelling read."

Rob Jacobs
Fellowship of Christian Athletes, Southcoastal Area
Director of South Carolina

With love from: Kristy Noel Gillinder

A Beautiful Mess

Life's painful messes birth beautiful blessings...
(Inspired by true events)

Kristy Noel Gillinder

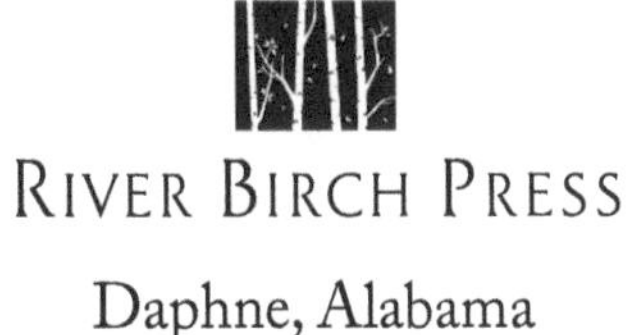

River Birch Press
Daphne, Alabama

A Beautiful Mess by Kristy Noel Gillinder

ISBN 978-1-956365-21-4 (print)
ISBN 978-1-956365-22-1 (e-book)

For Worldwide Distribution
Printed in the U.S.A.

River Birch Press
P.O. Box 868, Daphne, AL 36526

Dedication

First and foremost, to God: You loved me when I was unlovable. You forgive me even though I don't deserve it. You extend grace and mercy to me on a daily basis. You have blessed me beautifully, far beyond my wildest dreams. Thank You, Lord. I love You.

To Rob: You are God's match for me in every way. I truly can't imagine my life without you. You comfort me, you challenge me, you support me, and you make me laugh every single day. And you are one handsome fella. I love you.
Song of Solomon 8:6-7

To Bella: I am so proud to be your mom. I love seeing the hard-working and creative young woman you are becoming. You are so strong. May Jesus fill your heart every day. I love you.
Proverbs 3:5-6 and Proverbs 22:6

To Noah: You are a unique soul. Don't ever let that change. I am so glad to be your mom. May you walk closely with God always. Thank you for making me laugh. I love you.
Deuteronomy 31:6 and Proverbs 22:6

To Jeannette Vivas Soto: Thank you for sticking with me through it all. You are a loyal and loving friend, the sister I always wanted but never had. I love you.
Proverbs 18:24

In loving memory of : Mitzi Flowers Williams: You were a true friend, and I look forward to hugging you in heaven. I love and miss you.
Philippians 1:3

To Gina Renay Meyer: You are an amazing woman. I am blessed by your friendship and encouragement. I love how God sends just the right people into our lives at just the right time. You always make me think about Hebrews 13:2. I love you.

To Cary Russell Nelsen: You bring me so much joy. You have taught me so much about loving Jesus, and living for Him in all parts of my life. You are the sister of my heart. I love you.
Philippians 1:3

To Lana Reed: You are such a delight to my soul. Thank you for being a beloved part of my life. I love you.
Philippians 1:3

To Paola Vargas: When I found bloombellamoda.com, I didn't just find a great boutique and wonderful stylist, I found an amazing friend. I am thankful for you. I love you.
Psalm 34:8

To Arden Rose, Blake Robert, and Danielle Faith: Mommy loves and misses you, and I look forward to being with you in heaven.
Philippians 1:3

To Tonya Sue Sykes: I treasure your friendship. I love you.
Philippians 1:3

To Brittney Huegel: You are such blessing to me. I love you and Gracen.
Philippians 1:3

To Becky Ann Burns: Thank you for your constant encouragement. I love you.
Philippians 1:3

To Candy Davis Milam: You help me keep going no matter what. I love you.
Philippians 1:3

To Pat Calhoun: You are an amazing mentor and friend. I love you.
Philippians 1:3

To Megan Carlen: Thank you for helping me find the laughter in each day. I love you. Philippians 1:3

To Keith Carroll: Thank you for believing in me and supporting me.
Ecclesiastes 4:12

1

"Why doesn't anyone want to play with me? Doesn't anybody love me?" Danielle Laurel Graden wondered aloud. Once again, she was playing alone with her numerous dolls, her only friends. The five-year-old was amazingly intuitive for a youngster, seeing things that people many times her age often couldn't grasp.

Rain threatened again, like it always did, during the summers in the mountains of North Carolina.

Danni's grandmother, Ruby, came and scooped her up into her still-strong arms. "It's gonna rain, child," she chided. "Did you want to stay out here and let the rain monster melt you away?" There was a veiled gleam in her bright green eyes. Ruby was a short woman with perfectly styled gray hair that was never out of place. She was the kind of woman who never purposely got her hands dirty.

Hints of some evil force never ceased to frighten Danni out of her wits, and this time was no exception. "No! No!" Danni wailed pitifully. "Please don't let him take me away!" She sobbed into her grandmother's shoulder, clinging tightly, afraid but not quite sure of what.

Ruby deposited Danni on the blue chintz sofa in the small, wood-paneled living room. Danni's mother, Iris, was sitting in Danni's favorite rocking chair, mending Danni's blue denim shirt.

"Danni, I don't know how you manage to keep poking holes in your clothes," Iris sighed as she wiped away a bead of sweat from her wrinkled forehead. Her miserable expression and tired posture made her look far older than her forty years. Iris was an unhappy woman. Her daughter was said to be the very soul of her existence, but lately, Iris wasn't acting like it. She wasn't acting like herself at all, and she was reaching the point of not even caring.

Iris was once a beautiful woman who could have had her choice of eligible young suitors. She had been popular in school, involved in all the "right" clubs and activities, and made good grades. She was the daughter any parent should be proud of, but hers were anything but typical parents. Her Cherokee mother married her father after she discovered she was almost four months pregnant.

They fought incessantly, and Iris was used by both parents for their own selfish purposes. Her father made her cook and clean like she was a maid, and her mother made her care for her five younger siblings. Nothing Iris ever did was praised or rewarded. If she displeased either parent, a good hard slap and a stream of obscenities were her rewards.

When Iris was sixteen-years-old, she met Joseph Callaphoni and soon fell in love. Joseph was from a wealthy Italian family and had a bright future. Joseph and Iris dreamed of running away together and getting married. Iris, at last, had found someone to love her until the day that shattered her world.

Joseph was killed when a drunk driver plowed into his car, fled the scene, and was never caught. Iris never truly recovered from the loss of Joseph. Finally, her best friend, Carol, introduced Iris to her fiancé's cousin, Kurt, who wasn't like the boys at her school. He certainly wasn't like Joseph, and that made him appealing. All Iris wanted to do was escape and forget her loss of Joseph.

Kurt was twenty and had money, a job, and a fancy red car. These were just the sort of things that a lonely teenage girl would find appealing. Kurt lived with his mother, as his father had long since abandoned the family and returned home to his native Germany. They seemed to be a happy family, making Iris long to be with them.

Iris finally broke down and told Kurt how her family treated her. "I don't think they know I'm alive, except they wouldn't have anyone to cook or clean or iron for them," Iris sobbed into Kurt's shoulder.

"Let's get married, then," Kurt said as he stubbed out his cigarette into the ashtray of his red Mustang. He blew out a steady stream of smoke as he made the suggestion with all the excitement and fanfare one would use in buying a new toothbrush.

For him, it was just another decision. For Iris, it was a lifeline, a second chance. It was like the opportunity that had been denied her with Joseph was being given to her again. She desperately clung to every word Kurt said.

"What about my scholarship to nursing school? One of the provisions is that I can't take it if I get married," Iris said, concerned. The idea of a college education had been her dream for as long as she could remember.

Kurt's face reddened in anger. "Well, what's it going to be? Me or school? You can't have both. It doesn't work that way."

Iris was taken aback by his temper. She knew he had a short fuse but was hoping that once they were married, it would go away. "You, of course," she answered quickly, wringing her hands.

"That's much better," Kurt said, sneering. Kurt didn't tell Iris, but Ruby had said it was time for him to get married, and he did everything she told him to. His mother was the most important person in Kurt's world, and he would have done anything to please her, no matter what.

"But, Mama, I want you to play dolls with me," Danni implored in a pitiful tone. Even though she knew she would get the same response, she wanted Mommy to pay attention to her just once in a while.

Realizing her mother was engrossed in her sewing and not paying any attention to her, Danni turned to her dolls. "The mommy and the daddy were going to have a baby, but the water took them away," Danni said as she acted out the story with her dolls. "The water is deep, and the water is cold. Everyone is afraid," she said in a haunting, sing-song voice.

Iris dropped her sewing, jumped up, and grabbed Danni by the shoulders, lifting her off the ground, causing Danni's doll family to tumble down. "That never happened! It was all just a dream. Do you hear me?" she was practically screaming as she continued to shake Danni.

Danni sobbed, and her tears came in waves as she said, "Yes, Mama. It never happened. It was all a dream."

"You know I don't have time for your nonsense. Your father will be here soon, and I have to have supper ready the minute he gets home. You remember that he works hard so we can afford to buy you all those foolish dolls and clothes that you are so good at tearing up."

With that hateful reply, Iris dropped Danni, who fell in a graceless heap, and Iris made her way to the kitchen, leaving Danni with Ruby and her omniscient smile.

"Grandma, will you please play with me?" Danni asked, looking at Ruby.

"No, dear, I think I will go read for a while." Ruby narrowed her eyes at Danni and strode out of the room, leaving Danni alone again. Ruby never intervened on Danni's behalf, and she never even checked to see if the little girl was okay.

A few minutes later, Danni heard the familiar sound of arguing coming from the kitchen. "You meddling old bat, can't you keep your nose out of our business?"

"You live in my house, and you'd do well to remember that. Everything that goes on here is my business," Ruby spat. "He is my son, and I know what is best for him!"

Danni hated hearing Iris and Ruby arguing. For that matter, she hated living with Ruby. She was always making Mama cry and causing some sort of trouble. The constant fighting made Danni's stomach upset.

Maybe the coming storm would bring lightning, make the house burn up, and she could run away. But, as soon as she had the thought, Danni knew it wasn't right to feel that way.

"Jesus will help me. He won't leave me alone here," Danni said aloud as she wrapped her arms around her knees and rocked back and forth as the thunder growled and rumbled closer and closer.

Just then, the front door opened, and a short, dark-haired man slunk in. Kurt Graden was nearly a full head shorter than Iris, but his cocky attitude made him think he was seven feet tall.

Ruby raced into the room, threw her arms around him, and said, "Welcome home! How was my boy's day?"

Kurt proceeded to go over the details of his monotonous day at the computer mill. Danni soon lost interest and retreated to her bedroom. At least there, she could feel sorry for herself in peace. She had forgotten that her dad was mad at her again. It had been at least a week since he'd blown up at something Danni had done.

"I wish I could remember what I'd done wrong this time, and then maybe Daddy would at least look at me," she said aloud.

After Iris called that dinner was ready, they all assembled around the table for a dinner of ham, potatoes, green beans, and biscuits. Iris had wiped her eyes, but they still looked red and puffy.

Danni wanted to crawl on her mother's lap and comfort her, but she knew no one in the house would allow, or even welcome, her gesture.

Iris asked Kurt, "How was your day, honey?"

Without even looking up from his plate, he answered laconically, "Fine." He then began sharing with Ruby about some juicy local gossip he had heard at work.

Iris stared at her plate and began shoveling food into her mouth. Usually, Kurt made snide remarks about the amount of food Iris ate, but tonight he was so engrossed in his conversation with Ruby that he didn't even bother making fun of Iris.

As soon as he finished eating, Kurt withdrew to lie down in front of the television in the living room and watch the evening news while Ruby watched from her favorite recliner. Iris cleaned up the kitchen while Danni helped. Iris had long since taught Danni not to ever bother Kurt when he was watching television. He got agitated if anybody messed with his routine. Danni had been reminded of that the hard way more than once, and she did not care to make that mistake again.

A couple of hours later, Iris helped Danni pick out what to wear for the annual Field Day at school the next day. Danni selected a cute denim shorts set that was just a bit too short.

"My goodness. Look how you're growing. I think a shopping trip to Belk's is in order for this weekend," a weary Iris said.

Danni clapped her hands together and shouted, "Thank you, Mama!"

"Hush!" Iris hissed. "You know Daddy will get mad if he finds out we spent any money. And you don't want any trouble, do you?" she asked, leaning in really close to Danni, so close Danni nearly choked on the stench of cigarette smoke that clung to every part of Iris.

Danni gulped in horror. "No, Mama. I don't want to get us in trouble," she replied.

Without another word, Iris turned away sadly and went to pack Kurt's lunch for the next day, but once again, Ruby had beaten her to it.

So, Iris just hid away in the corner with a book. Iris escaped through reading. She loved reading about people, other lands, wars, anything to get her mind off her own private mess. The funny thing was, in her personal war, she didn't even know whose side she landed on.

Meanwhile, Kurt got up and walked into Danni's room. "Hey," he said. And with his one-word greeting, he was signaling Danni, as he always did, that everything was forgiven, and that he would be on speaking terms with her until she made him angry again.

"Daddy, what did I do this time to make you mad?" Danni asked.

"With fists balled at his sides, Kurt's face reddened, and he punched Danni's shoulder. "You are stupid, just like your mother! I should be declared a saint for putting up with the two of you!" He spun on his heel, stalked to his bedroom, and slammed the door, leaving Danni to cry alone in her room.

Iris was afraid to tend to her, lest she find herself on the receiving end of one of Kurt's slaps or punches. Kurt knew just how hard to hit them, and where to hit them, so it wouldn't show. Iris and Danni were experts at hiding it.

Later, after everyone was asleep, Danni crept into the kitchen, got a chair, and carefully slid it over to the refrigerator. She climbed up and opened the top freezer part and removed a bag of frozen vegetables. She held it on her aching shoulder. After a while, the sharp cold numbed the pain. She replaced everything and went to bed, praying to Jesus to get her out of this mess.

At 11:30 p.m., Iris crept into Danni's room to check on her. Thankfully, she found her fast asleep with her favorite ragged stuffed bunny tucked under her arm. Iris didn't pray much, but this time she silently thanked God for sparing Danni from hearing the fight she'd had with Kurt. He'd punched her so hard in the stomach that she saw stars and vomited.

What Iris didn't know was that Danni had heard everything. Danni had been hiding outside their bedroom door and was nearly hit in the head when Kurt opened it in a fit of rage. Danni quickly retreated to her room and pretended to be asleep as she heard Kurt's tires squeal out of the driveway. She knew Iris would be in to check on her, and pretending to be asleep would be a way of escape.

At about three in the morning, Kurt stumbled in, dead drunk. He passed out, fully clothed and stinking, on top of his comforter. The family knew to leave him alone. Iris knew, as a dutiful wife, she would have to call his boss in a few hours and tell him Kurt was sick but would be back to work, hopefully, the following day. She knew the routine.

Somehow, both Danni and Iris made it through Field Day at Danni's school. Iris was a teacher's assistant, so she was never far away if Danni needed her during school hours. As Field Day ended, so did Danni's first year of school.

Finally, Danni had found somewhere she was wanted and could fit in. She loved learning and books and making new friends, and her teacher was the best. Nobody hit her or used ugly words there. She felt like she mattered. She loved going to school and church. As much as she liked school, church was her favorite. She loved hearing "Jesus stories." Jesus was her best friend, and Danni knew, someday, somehow, Jesus would get her out of the terrible mess at home.

To anyone outside the Graden home, they looked like the ideal family. Kurt was popular everywhere he went—at work, in the community, at church. He laughed and joked with everyone.

He was always the life of any social gathering. Meanwhile, Iris and Danni both just wanted to fade off into the corner and become a sad-looking pair of wallflowers.

However, Kurt simply wouldn't allow that. He made sure they were in the spotlight too but only on occasion. He didn't want anyone or anything tarnishing his reputation.

Everywhere they went, Danni heard the same thing. "Danni, your father is a saint. If he doesn't go to heaven, no one will." Those very words made her stomach turn over. No one outside their family knew what a strain it was to keep up appearances by making everything look and seem normal, when it was anything but normal.

2

Seventeen-year-old Danni was behind the wheel of the temperamental old Tempo. It wasn't much, but it was a set of wheels, and Danni was thankful to even have a car. Iris had grown even colder over the years. She was harsh, critical, and angry, and sometimes, Danni felt like acid just dripped from her mother's tongue. Iris harshly criticized everything Danni did. Danni drove too fast, she drove too slow, she followed cars too closely, she left too much space between cars, and the list seemed endless.

By the end of the forty-five minute trip to reach the mall, Danni was ready to yank out her long hair, and the tension showed on her face. She wanted to weep with sheer relief as she pulled into a parking space.

"Don't embarrass me," Iris hissed. "If you embarrass me in public, I will mash your mouth!"

"Fine, I will be a little angel for you," Danni said, in a rare moment of backtalk. She instantly knew she would regret that one later. Iris had taken to slapping Danni, sometimes while she was driving. Iris said that Danni had forced her to do it, and if they died in a car accident, they would both go to hell, and it would all be Danni's fault.

Iris and Danni shopped for several hours, looking for just the right dress for Danni's upcoming senior prom. Nothing pleased Iris. Nothing met with her stringent approval. As they wandered in and out of the shops, all Danni wanted was to lose herself in the throng of shoppers. To Danni, they all looked so happy and carefree. She longed to be with them, to be one of them.

"Danni, quit that stupid daydreaming. I should have known we'd never be able to find anything today," Iris said, yanking Danni's arm. "Let's go to Belk's and see what we can do about your makeup."

Danni was mortified. She had battled acne for the last couple of years. Kurt and Ruby, and finally Iris, had picked on her unmercifully about it. The kids at school were bad enough, but being made fun of at home was almost unbearable.

Thankfully, Iris had finally taken Danni to a doctor friend who put her on a strong medicine that actually worked. The side effect was it made her skin unusually dry, so the nickname "Alligator" was one she heard all too frequently.

At Belk's, Danni tried her best not to squirm as the perfect-skinned salesgirl sang the praises of a new makeup line that was "just divine" for women with dry, scaly skin.

On the way out of the mall, Iris spat, "Well, I hope you're happy with all the money I had to waste on you! We've fooled so much time we'll have to speed home so I can make dinner for Kurt. You heard the girl at Belk's, all you have to do is work a little harder to keep your skin clean and clear," Iris said with a smirk as they pulled out of the parking lot.

Danni had had enough. "No, all I need is some peace. Every time we have a fight or a blow-up at home, I get sick to my stomach and my face breaks out. Every single time, and you know it!"

Iris let out a string of obscenities that would have made a seasoned sailor blush. She slapped Danni across the mouth.

"You ungrateful idiot! You have it made and don't even know it," Iris spat. With trembling hands, she pulled out a cigarette from her purse, lit it, and began puffing away. She chain-smoked all the way home, while Danni's hands shook at the wheel. Danni prayed they wouldn't get into an accident. The smoke smell made her dizzy and nauseous, but Iris didn't care.

When they finally arrived home, Kurt was sprawled out in front of the television, mindlessly watching the local news, while Ruby was daintily perched on her favorite chair.

Danni immediately fled to her room, while Iris was ignored by Kurt yet again.

"Have you had dinner yet?" Iris asked hopefully.

"Don't worry about it," Kurt snarled. "Ruby already made me something to eat." With that, he went back to watching television after turning up the volume, signaling an end to Iris's attempt at conversation.

Half an hour later, Iris knocked on Danni's door and told her it was time to eat. They had their meal, just the two of them, while the others stayed glued to their posts in the living room.

Danni's stomach lurched again. It was no wonder she had digestive issues and skin problems. The stress was too much for her. She had worked extra hard in school and had applied for every possible scholarship. She should be hearing back any day now. She felt like this was God's way of getting her out. Danni knew He wouldn't leave her here forever.

After dinner, Danni hurried to the bathroom and cleaned her face again. "Tomorrow, it will clear up. Tomorrow it will get better," she said as she methodically cleaned her face with an almost religious zeal. She washed and buffed and shined until she was satisfied.

Then, she carefully applied her makeup, which was getting easier and easier to do. She used a light foundation, a lovely pink blush, three shades of eye shadow, and some finishing powder. Danni was nearly six feet tall, with long, strawberry blonde hair, and high cheekbones. The makeup minimized her skin troubles, and highlighted her huge green eyes. She topped it all off with a hint of pink lipstick. Although she was pretty, all she could hear were the voices of Kurt, Ruby, and even Iris pointing out her flaws.

Iris came to find her a little later. She slipped her some money. "Your father would kill me if he knew I was giving you this. I don't know what young people really like. I'm so old I don't even know what the latest styles are. You and Beth go find something pretty, okay?"

Danni quickly tucked the money away and said, "Thanks, Mom. We will."

School was out for a teachers' workday the next day, so Danni had made plans to hit the mall that afternoon with her best friend, Beth Bradley. Beth was an absolute lifesaver to Danni.

Beth's parents were so warm and welcoming, and everything her family wasn't. Even Beth's aggravating little sister, Jenny, was a welcome addition to Danni's life. Beth and her family attended the same church as the Gradens, and Beth and Danni were in youth group together, which they both loved.

Danni did her best to put Kurt, Ruby, and Iris out of her mind as she rolled along in the battered old Tempo and made her way down Highway 301 South. She lost herself in the music from the radio as she drove through the dark green hills, dotted here and there with prime pasture and grazing land for cows and horses. Danni smiled as she thought about how peaceful the land looked.

As she pulled up to Beth's parents' two-story Tudor-style home, Danni felt a slight twinge of envy, not at the beautiful home, but the love she always felt glowing within. She sighed softly as she turned off the engine and got out of her car. Freckles, the Bradleys' goofy and lovable little mutt, greeted her with two furry paws firmly planted on her kneecaps. That was about as high as he could reach. Danni desperately wanted a dog of her own, so Freckles was a bit like her adopted dog, at least in her heart.

Freckles disappeared around the corner, probably to chase a rabbit, or even worse, a skunk. Danni couldn't help thinking that this home was a castle with its round turrets on the second floor and its elaborate, walled garden courtyard with a center-style fountain. She and Beth had spent many hours in the courtyard, throwing water from the fountain on each other, planning their future careers, either as major movie stars or rock stars, of course, and dreaming of their future husbands.

Beth had been going steady with Andy Johnson, the only son of the town librarian and town sheriff, since they were in fourth grade. He was everyone's hero, captain of the football team, and had given his life to Jesus in the sixth grade. Andy had been talking about becoming a minister since he was in ninth grade and said he intended to marry Beth someday. Danni was only sorry Andy didn't have a twin brother for her!

Danni smiled at the flood of fond memories as she rang the doorbell. She was greeted by Linda, Beth's mother. Linda was wearing a blue, floor-length silk dress and sapphire and diamond earrings. A matching bracelet and necklace helped complete her enchanting look. The jewels were a fortieth birthday present for Linda, who didn't even mind hitting that important milestone year a few months ago.

Danni guessed correctly that Linda and Beth's father were going to an important event for his company, Bradley Research, Inc., a highly lucrative company that dealt with plastics research and development.

As a result of her husband's successful business, Linda was able to quit her job as a twelfth-grade history teacher and devote herself to her husband and daughters full-time. It was a blessing they were all grateful for. The family was even closer now, and they said they wouldn't trade that for anything. They were quick to give God the praise for it, and it warmed Danni's heart to hear it.

Ever the consummate hostess, Linda ushered Danni inside and asked, "How are you, Danni?"

"I'm fine, thanks," Danni said, smiling.

Linda offered Danni a seat, explaining that Beth was helping Jenny clean up after she had given Jenny a cooking lesson. Their father, Daniel, was supervising the loading of the dishwasher while all decked out in his tux.

As Linda chatted on about their prom preparations, Danni nodded her head politely, trying to keep up with the conversation as she glanced around the familiar living room again. The floor of the two-story foyer was covered with large, heavy stones imported from England.

The sunken living room, where they were currently sitting, featured a massive stone fireplace, several large paintings from well-known artists, and some lovely French antiques adorning the room. A huge bay window allowed them to see the stars and enjoy the nighttime view. They had no nearby neighbors, so all they could see was the countryside, which suited them beautifully.

A few minutes later, the rest of the Bradley brood rounded the corner. Little six-year-old Jenny was wearing an adorable pink Osh Kosh b'Gosh outfit. She was missing two front teeth, and her little grin was too cute for words.

Danni playfully ruffled Jenny's hair, and Jenny flashed her toothless grin, which made Danni's heart happy. Danni was like another well-loved child for Linda and Daniel. Although they were wealthy materially, they didn't care about that. They appreciated it, of course, but people mattered more to them than stuff ever would.

They were the kind of people who made you feel good about life just being around them, and Danni needed all of that she could get. The Bradleys didn't care that Danni drove a beat-up old car that backfired often, or that she lived in a one-hundred-year-old farmhouse that was shabbily fixed up. All they cared about was that Danni was a true friend to Beth and always had been.

Beth was tall—not as tall as Danni but tall nonetheless. She had thick, curly black hair, green eyes, and freckles. Jenny had suggested they named their dog Freckles in honor of her beloved sister, and everyone had agreed.

Ever since she was young, Beth had struggled with her weight. She wasn't exactly overweight but was just a bit bigger than she wanted to be. And, just like Danni got picked on for her acne, Beth got picked on for her size. Somehow, it bonded Beth and Danni even more, and they supported each other. They were each other's most faithful prayer warrior.

Just then, the doorbell rang, and Daniel answered it. When he returned, Mrs. Browne, Jenny's delightful babysitter, was with him. She was a wonderful, older English lady who had been a nanny for a couple in London and had relocated to Asheville, North Carolina. She was semi-retired now but loved to babysit for Jenny anytime the Bradleys needed her.

Linda and Daniel bade everyone a good evening and left for their gala event. Danni, Beth, and Jenny waved from the enormous front door. Jenny took Mrs. Browne's hand and led the way to the kitchen in search of some chocolate chip cookies.

As Danni and Beth were backing out of Beth's driveway, Danni grinned ruefully at the incongruous picture her old car made next to Beth's home and even her Mazda Miata, which had been a sixteenth birthday present from her parents. But, like her parents, Beth couldn't have cared less about stuff and Danni loved her for it.

As they made their way to the mall, Danni asked Beth to tell her the story just one more time.

"Okay, okay." Beth grinned. "Here goes. The handsome Englishman, Daniel Bradley, came to the International Business

School at Duke University. There he met a pretty country lass named Linda, who was on scholarship to study history. She was delighted by his good looks and fine manners. He, in turn, was charmed by her accent, strong values, and beauty. She is the one who introduced him to Jesus, and the rest, as they say, is history!"

Danni grinned. "That is so sweet and romantic, it makes my teeth hurt."

Both girls giggled as they turned their attention to some serious prom shopping. Beth didn't tell Danni about the conversation she and Linda had had earlier that day. Linda knew, in her heart, that something just wasn't right at Danni's home. She couldn't put her finger on it, exactly, but she just knew something was off. She didn't want to pry, but the entire Bradley family loved Danni like one of their own, and they were concerned about her.

The Bradleys didn't think anyone would make a big fuss over the prom for her as Beth would receive, so Linda suggested they go shopping together. Linda and Daniel decided to stay in the background a bit, so they called up the girls' favorite stores at the mall and told them to take good care of both Beth and Danni.

When the girls arrived at the mall, they found a great parking spot and were soon shopping happily. They had a grand time trying on all sorts of dresses. They laughed and joked and gave each other good, honest advice. They each wanted the other to look and feel her best on such a special night, so they took great care in helping each other find something extra special. Beth finally settled on a floor-length, sky blue gown with simple lines. It was perfect.

"Bethy, Andy will positively drool over you in this!" Danni exclaimed, genuinely happy for her friend.

Beth blushed and replied, "And Russell will faint when he sees you."

Danni's dress was a deep purple silk shantung with elegant

curves and folds. It was stunning. She grinned as she and Beth pirouetted in front of the wall of mirrors in the dressing area.

When they prepared to leave the dressing area, Beth quietly told Danni her parents were taking care of everything. "Thank you, but I've got this. It's okay," Danni replied. She was relieved when Beth didn't pursue it.

Next, they selected their dyed-to-match shoes and then decided that, after a very successful prom shopping trip, they'd go home and call their respective dates.

Danni dropped Beth off with a wave and headed home. When she got home, Ruby was out for the evening. Kurt had gone to bed, and Iris was reading a book.

"Hi, Mom," Danni said as she brought in her purchases.

"What did you find?" Iris asked.

Danni carefully laid out the treasured dress in its garment bag and unzipped it. Iris nodded her approval when Danni pulled it out and asked her to try it on for her.

Iris didn't really praise her but again nodded her approval, which was the best Danni could hope for. She said good-night to Iris, changed, and hung up the dress reverently in the back of her closet, tucked carefully inside the garment bag. Danni prayed it would be protected from the smell of cigarette smoke. It was so nauseating and embarrassing for everything to have that nasty smell clinging to it.

Danni washed her face, carefully following her recommended routine, and then called Russell, who was her oldest friend besides Beth.

"Hey there. How are you?" Danni asked.

"I'm great. How are you?" Russell inquired. If there was one thing Russell didn't fail on, it was manners. He was so kind and polite that people just were naturally drawn to him. He was really cute too, so Danni always thought it was a shame that she loved

Russell like a brother and nothing else. She really wanted to like him, but it just wasn't meant to be. That didn't keep Russell from hoping, though.

"Beth and I picked out our dresses and accessories tonight. I got a fabric swatch for us to match your cummerbund and bow tie. When do you want to meet so we can go and reserve your tux?" Danni asked.

A little too quickly, Russell suggested, "How about Sunday after church? We can have lunch with my family, and then go and take care of it. How does that sound?"

"Great, as a matter of fact," Danni smiled into the phone. Russell had a wonderful family. The Camerons reminded her of Beth's family to a great extent. Russell's father, Jim Cameron, was the minister of their church. A kindly man in his forties, he still had the youthful good looks that he had carried onto Mountainview High's football field some twenty-odd years before.

Russell's mother, Laura, truly was a superwoman. Only three short years before, she had been diagnosed with breast cancer, and after a double mastectomy and difficult treatments, she thought she would be fine. Scarcely a year after her final treatment, the cancer had returned. They were facing the battle bravely, and Laura refused to alter their lifestyle any more than was absolutely necessary. She was too devoted to her husband and Russell and little seven-year-old Zach. She had given up her job at the local bank, but other than that, she refused to change. She was happy with her life, and she believed that by staying strong and continuing to fight, God would heal her.

Danni was a bit nervous eating around other people because of her constant stomach turmoil at her own family mealtimes. But she figured she could use the practice of eating somewhere other than home before prom night. She was very comfortable with Russell and his family, so she was looking forward to being with them.

They said goodnight, hung up, and Danni went to bed. She grinned as she went to sleep and dreamed about the upcoming prom. It was going to be so much fun!

Saturday flew by as Danni worked on her homework and helped Iris around the house, and before she knew it, it was Sunday. Danni dressed carefully for church, as she always did. Today, she selected an emerald green, knee-length dress and coordinating heels. She wore tiny green earrings.

At precisely nine-thirty, Kurt announced, "Time to go." That was his way of exercising his authority. He grinned as he issued stern statements or barked orders like a drill sergeant. He and Ruby took his Mustang to church while Danni and Iris took her Tempo. Danni prayed it would make it there and back safely. The rattling and backfiring were definitely getting worse.

The church service was touching, as always. Pastor Jim truly had a heart for God and people, and it showed in his lessons. Today's lesson was all about being prepared for the hereafter. Danni sat with Russell and his family, who were right behind the Bradleys. Iris sat in the choir section, which was mostly filled with seniors and widows, and Kurt nodded off to sleep on the back row, while Ruby primly say nearby. If anyone ever got too close to the Graden family, Kurt would make veiled comments that Iris was "a little off" or that she was "going through the change" as if that explained everything.

After church, Danni enjoyed a lively lunch with Russell's family. Theirs was a home full of laughter and love and sticking together through the triumphs and tragedies of life. Their well-loved little ranch home was like a welcoming hug for Danni's heart. After they ate and visited, Danni and Russell took care of his tuxedo rental, and everything was all set for prom.

That night, a huge storm rocked the Graden house. It felt like the entire world was shaking. Danni had never liked storms, or being in the dark, anyway, but this middle-of-the night storm was a particular doozy. Lightning flashed and lit up her bedroom window like it was the middle of the day.

All of a sudden, she heard the doorknob on her flimsy little door turning. Although the door did little in the way of protecting her from a midnight beating, Danni liked to think the idea of a locked door offered her at least a bit of safety.

She'd been so happy today that she wasn't paying enough attention when she went to bed to remember to lock the door. Now, it opened and Kurt was standing in the hallway, just outside her door. The lightning flashed and illuminated his sick grin. Danni forgot to pretend to be asleep. Her eyes opened wide when he waved his hand.

She saw he was holding a gun. He aimed it at her and said, "Bang! Bang!" He then laughed, slammed the door, and she heard his footsteps retreating down the hall. The thunder blocked out everything else.

Danni couldn't stop shaking. She waited for what seemed like forever until she crept out of bed. She stealthily went to retrieve a garbage bag and changed her clothes and the sheets on her bed. As she hid the soiled items in the back of her closet, she prayed she would quickly have an opportunity to wash them before anyone discovered Kurt had scared her so badly that she'd wet her bed. The shame and sorrow of it all made her face burn.

3

Danni was thankful for the ritual of her school schedule. School and church were the only places Kurt and Iris and Ruby couldn't do anything to her. She would gladly take the name-calling and teasing from the other kids about her height and acne over the Gradens' unpredictable behavior any day of the week.

On her way home after school Monday afternoon, Danni checked the mail. The mailbox was almost half a mile from her house, so she swung the Tempo over, hopped out, and took a peek to see if any worthwhile mail had arrived. She pulled out a stack of bills, advertisements, and assorted junk mail.

She had almost given up hope when something made her take one more look. Crumpled up in the back corner of the mailbox was what she had been praying so hard for—a letter from the University of the Carolinas at Charlotte. She was shaking so hard she could barely open it. Twice, she dropped it. On the third attempt, tears blurred her eyes as she saw the congratulatory greeting at the top. The full scholarship she had prayed and worked so hard for was hers!

She couldn't believe it. "Lord, thank You. Oh, thank You. I won't take this for granted," she promised as she buried her head against the steering wheel and gave in to her range of emotions. She had been praying for a way of escape for a long time. She knew God was listening, and now He was delivering her.

That night, a storm of rage was unleashed, the likes of which Danni had never seen. When Danni announced her scholarship over dinner, Iris cried, claiming that Danni didn't love her and was abandoning her. Kurt cursed, threw his bowl of stew on the floor, and punched Danni's shoulder.

He stormed from the room, and Ruby followed him, after icily calling over her shoulder, "You ungrateful brat! After all that my son has done for you, all you want to do is just leave here like we are trash to you. I hid that letter in the back of the mailbox in the hope that you wouldn't find it."

Ruby then dramatically swept from the room, presumably to go and comfort her son. The entire scene had a soap opera feel and would have been funny had it not been Danni's actual real life. That just made it all so very pathetic.

As expected, Danni's stomach knotted up. She vomited, losing the little bit of food she had been able to eat. She barely slept that night, and her face was beginning to break out by the next morning. She said not one word to any of them and left for school as soon as possible.

To her surprise, right after homeroom, a huge assembly was called in the gym. Her favorite teacher, Mr. Palmer, called the group to order. He announced the senior class's scholarship winners. Danni turned out to have received the most prestigious one.

She blushed furiously at the thunderous applause, and Beth, Russell, and Andy went nuts, cheering and fist-pumping and hugging her until she felt like a squeezed melon. She didn't mind, though, because this felt a whole world away from how things were at home.

The next three weeks flew by in a flurry of preparations for college and prom. And then, finally, prom day arrived. Danni thought she would faint from excitement. Her father and Ruby both managed to be away all day, which suited Danni just fine. Iris was coming to terms with Danni leaving soon. Kurt still hadn't "forgiven" Danni, and neither had Ruby, but Danni was past caring what they thought anymore.

Danni and Iris went to the best hairstylist in town. She curled Danni's long hair and swept it up into a dramatic up-do, leaving a few tendrils to curl around her face. Once home, Danni painted her nails a shimmering silver.

Beth called Danni four times. "Daddy says he will never live until Jenny goes to her first prom!" Beth giggled.

"Why not?" Danni asked.

"He says I will either talk him to death or worry him into a retirement home," Beth explained. She erupted into a fit of laughter and Danni joined her. "Okay, I've got to go. See you in a few hours," Beth said, and then hung up.

Danni walked into the living room. There was still no sign of Kurt or Ruby, and she was glad. She was hoping Iris would want to take some pictures, but instead she was pulling out a cigarette and lighter. "Mom, you promised you'd wait until we left, please," Danni pleaded.

Iris made a face and slammed everything onto a nearby table. "Fine, but you'd better hurry. You're getting on my nerves," she said, scowling.

Danni prayed for calm as she looked out the window. Mercifully, Russell was right on time, as always. He parked and hurried to the front door. He didn't even have a chance to ring the doorbell before Danni swept it open.

"Wow, Danni, you look beautiful!" Russell exclaimed.

"You don't look so bad yourself," Danni replied.

Turning his attention to Iris, Russell said, "Hi, Mrs. Graden. How are you?"

"I'm fine," she sighed. "I'm sure you two want to get going. Have a great night," she said.

Momentarily taken aback by her abruptness, which was so

different from his family, Russell quickly recovered. "Of course. Thank you. Have a good night, Mrs. Graden."

Danni hurried out the door to the station wagon, which Russell had borrowed for the evening. He opened the door for her and helped her inside. They soon relaxed on the drive over to Beth's house. Once there, he handed her a lovely corsage of purple alstroemerias, miniature white roses, and baby's breath.

"Thank you. It's beautiful!" Danni exclaimed, giving him a hug.

Linda and Daniel opened the door and crowed over Russell and Danni. They joined Beth and Andy, who were in the middle of the living room. Andy positively glowed as he looked at Beth. He'd pretty much looked at her that way since the day his family moved to town when they were all in the fourth grade. Andy's dad was elected sheriff the very next year, and the year after that, his mom left her job at the high school to become the town librarian.

They adored Beth and her family and were hopeful Beth would join their family someday. Andy was just over six feet tall. He had curly, strawberry blonde hair that got out of control every summer. He and Beth made a beautiful couple.

After what seemed like an eternity of posing for pictures, they were finally in the limo and on their way to dinner. They had decided to make a reservation at Annabel's, and it was perfect. They laughed and talked and enjoyed each other's company, along with some great food.

After dinner, they continued the party on the way to the prom. The theme was "Island of Paradise" and a festive luau theme really helped get the party started. Everyone danced and laughed and had a wonderful time. They each knew the memories they were making were precious.

Andy held Beth close every chance he got, and she couldn't stop smiling.

Danni and Russell danced a lot but also enjoyed sitting and talking. They never had trouble talking to each other.

All too soon, it was time to go home. Danni felt a bit like Cinderella going back to the dungeon of her life after the ball. They waved to their friends and classmates who were piling into cars and trucks and station wagons and limos. Everyone agreed it had been a success.

Once in the limo, Beth held out her hand and announced, "Andy gave me a promise ring!"

Danni and Russell were quick to congratulate them, and they were all ecstatic. The ride back to Beth's house was almost an hour long, so they had plenty of time to laugh and joke and make plans about their futures, which all felt bright.

Suddenly, the limo driver began screaming, but no one could understand what he was shouting. Everything happened so fast. The limo was hit by what felt like a train. Glass and metal shattered into millions of pieces and rained down everywhere. The car flipped end-over-end and kept rolling as it broke apart and finally came to rest on its roof. The last sound anyone heard was Danni's ear-piercing wail.

Russell was strapped in by his seat belt and was upside down. The seat belt was stuck fast and wouldn't budge. He couldn't move but could feel something hot and wet oozing down his face. He called out the others' names but was met with an eerie silence.

"Help us! Help us! Please, God, please send help!" Russell screamed.

Not one to panic easily, Russell kept praying and breathing deeply to slow his racing heart. He fought to regain control over his emotions. He worked and squirmed and finally, with the use of broken shards of glass, he sawed his way through the seat belt and managed to cut himself free of his restraint. He landed in a heap but didn't care. All he could think of was finding his friends and helping them.

Russell fumbled around until he felt a body. He wasn't able to see who it was, so he just held on and crawled through a nearby window, pulling them with him. He soon realized it was Danni. Russell laid her on the ground and was relieved to find her still breathing.

He crawled back into the car and found Andy next. Andy was a big, strong guy but so was Russell. Once Russell got him out, he was met with incoherent groaning. It was obvious that both of his legs were badly crushed.

Russell went back in for Beth next. He kept calling her name over and over and heard nothing. Then, the realization dawned. The sunroof was open and Beth had been leaning in to show them her promise ring just before the accident. He crawled back out and began searching. He found her about fifty feet from where the car had finally landed on its roof. He knew as soon as he saw her that she was already dead. He dropped to his knees and sobbed as he covered her with his jacket.

Russell stumbled back to the limo one last time to search for the driver. He was still strapped inside, and he was dead too.

Russell searched until he found a cell phone in the wreckage and called for help. While checking on his friends, he realized that they had been hit by a bright red Jeep Cherokee. With a sickening pounding in his chest, Russell looked inside and saw one of their classmates, who came from a family with a history of drinking problems, dead behind the steering wheel. The overwhelming fumes of alcohol made him sick. He stumbled backward and vomited.

Andy's father was first on the scene. He was barely able to hold it together as he realized what had happened. Four ambulances arrived, along with a whole host of emergency personnel. Lights and sirens and sounds and smells were everywhere. Everyone who was there that night knew that they would never be the same.

Russell's family met them at the hospital. Andy's father had picked up his wife and came in right behind Russell's family. Russell was bruised and severely traumatized but otherwise would be fine.

The Johnsons were just glad Andy was alive. "The damage to his legs is extensive. He will need several surgeries to make sure he can walk properly," the doctor said. "I know he was counting on that football scholarship, but that is out of the question now."

Linda Johnson sobbed, "I'm just glad he's alive. We can deal with everything else later." Sheriff Johnson nodded sagely, tears streaming unchecked down his face.

When news that Beth had been pronounced dead at the scene was delivered, everyone was devastated. None of them could even begin to process the reality that the sweet, beautiful girl with curly hair and freckles and contagious laughter was no longer alive.

4

Meanwhile, Iris had arrived at the hospital with Kurt and Ruby in tow. "How is she?" Iris asked the doctor.

"Danielle is a very blessed girl. She looked a lot worse than she actually is when she first arrived. She broke her arm and has a concussion. She lost a fair amount of blood from multiple lacerations but not enough to be in danger. We want to keep her overnight for observation. After that, she can go home," the doctor explained.

"Thank God," Iris said. "Danni hadn't been drinking, had she?"

The doctor looked at Iris quizzically for a moment, then replied, "No. Nothing at all showed up on any of her blood tests. Why do you ask?"

Iris shifted uncomfortably, unable to admit that her husband and mother-in-law had badgered her all the way to the hospital to ask that question. They were always in terrible fear that somehow their family would be embarrassed or shamed in any given situation. Not one time on the drive to the hospital had anyone said anything about being worried about Danni.

"No reason, in particular," Iris replied. "When can I see her?"

The doctor caught the "I" and not "we" but decided not to pursue it further. "You can see her now."

Iris said, "Let's go." The doctor led the way, and Ruby and Kurt followed at a distance.

Iris cried quietly as she looked at her daughter. Danni was

asleep when they entered. Her left arm was heavily bandaged from her fingertips to her shoulder. Iris assumed the bandages were to protect the heavy cast underneath. Danni's head was wrapped in a large white bandage, and her left eye was swollen shut. She looked like a limp rag doll.

Finally, Danni stirred. "Mama, what happened?"

Iris's eyes quickly sought out the doctor's, who quietly nodded his head.

"You and your friends were in an accident. You are in the hospital, but you are going to be just fine," he said.

"Where are my friends? Are they okay?" Danni asked with a terrible, sinking feeling.

The doctor stepped in once he realized Iris was struggling with what to say. He said, "Andrew is going to be a few doors down, and Russell is fine."

"But...what about Bethy?" Danni asked, trying to pull herself up. Kurt and Ruby had already stepped out of the room, once they realized Danni was going to be okay, leaving Iris and the doctor to tell Danni that, in an instant, her whole world had changed and that absolutely nothing would ever be the same for her.

Just then, Russell walked in, followed by his parents, and he began to cry when he saw Danni. It was in that moment that Danni knew Beth was gone.

"No!" Danni wailed pitifully.

Pastor Jim, who always had a delicate touch, moved closer, and with tears in his eyes, said, "Honey, Beth is with God now."

"I don't believe you," Danni said, sobbing openly. "She was just sitting with me in the car. She is *not* dead. She can't be. She just can't be!" Beth was not only Danni's best friend, she was her sister in Christ and an endless source of encouragement and support for her.

Everyone crowded around Danni's bed, trying to help her comprehend what had happened, desperate to console her.

Pastor Jim said, "Danni, it is awful. We are all heartbroken. This is a time when we need to lean on each other, to get through this."

Linda Cameron gently laid one hand on her husband's shoulder and laid her other hand on Danni's unbroken arm. "We can't get through this, but God will carry us through it."

Pastor Jim began praying, "Lord, our hearts are just broken. We don't understand. We don't pretend that we do. All we know is that we love You, and we know You love us. Please carry us through this loss. We thank You for the time we had with Beth. Please surround her family and loved ones with Your tender mercies and healing. Please blanket us in Your peace that surpasses all understanding. Turn it all out for good in a way that only You can. We thank You for Danni and Andy and Russell still being with us. Please heal them from the inside out. We thank You for never changing, for never leaving us, not even for a moment. We thank You that Beth is home with You now, and for the assurance that we will be with her again. We love You, dear Lord. In the precious name of Jesus we pray. Amen."

For long moments, no one spoke. A gentle hush fell over the room. God was there in the silence. They felt Him in each breath, in each heartbeat. And, although their hearts were broken, they had hope, the kind of hope that comes in knowing that God is already in tomorrow, and that He has a plan.

Iris pulled up a chair to sit with Danni for a few minutes. Russell and his parents said good-night and made their way to see Andy's parents. Andy was still in surgery and was expected to be there for several more hours, according to the head nurse.

Danni fell asleep and Iris left quietly. She hurried out to the parking lot where Kurt and Ruby were waiting. "What took you so long?" Kurt asked, while impatiently stubbing out a cigarette. Iris crawled into the backseat, trying not to get in Ruby's way. For once, she didn't care. Iris just sat staring numbly out the window as she reached into her battered purse, looking for a cigarette of her own.

When Russell got home, he hugged his parents and went to his bathroom to shower. For the first time since the accident, he took a look at himself in the mirror. He had become a man in one heartbreaking night. His clothes were covered in blood, and most of it was not his.

He grabbed an empty bag, jammed everything in it, tied it in a firm knot, and stuffed it in the bottom of his garbage can. Russell knew he would be ill if he ever had to look at any of those clothes again. He would gladly pay any fees from the tux shop. Everything was ruined anyway.

After a long, hot shower and more prayer, Russell tried to sleep. As physically exhausted as he was, his mind just wouldn't shut down. He envied Danni just a bit. The doctor had insisted on giving her something to make her sleep. With the amount of pain from her broken arm, Russell was sure she needed it. The doctors had offered Russell something, but he had declined and now was wondering if he should have asked for something after all.

Four days later, over a thousand people showed up at Mountainview Non-Denominational Church. It was a brilliantly sunny day, Beth's favorite kind. People were stuffed like sardines inside the church. Those who couldn't fit inside stood in the parking lot, and still others lined both sides of the street to say goodbye to an amazing young woman who was so clearly loved. Beth had stood up to people who bullied her about her size. She had stood up for Danni. She had stood up for what was right, and she had made such a beautiful, lasting impression on people's hearts that not even death could taint it. People turned out in droves to honor Beth and what she had represented.

In comparison, the teenage drunk driver and fellow classmate of Beth, the one who had caused the fatal accident, had a small, graveside service, attended by only four people. Daniel and Linda Bradley, in a supreme act of forgiveness, offered to pay for the girl's funeral, but her mother had refused and even cursed them. It was all they could do to hold themselves up and walk away, but they did.

Jim Cameron knew that this was an opportunity to share the Good News of Jesus, and to talk about forgiveness and moving forward in hope and love. He was up most of the night before the funeral, praying for God's guidance. He wanted it to be God's words flowing into people's ears and not his. Jim prayed to be an instrument to point people to Jesus, and that was exactly what happened. There wasn't a dry eye anywhere to be had.

Although it took nothing short of a superhero effort to be there, Andy was in the front row with Beth's family. Danni was there too and couldn't stop shaking.

As soon as the service was over, Andy had to return to the hospital. He was facing multiple surgeries to regain the fullest possible recovery for both of his legs. His parents, with his blessing, had decided to move the family back to their native Los Angeles. He didn't think he could bear to be here without expecting to see Beth around every corner. It was just too painful.

So, as soon as arrangements could be made, they were leaving. Although they had lived in Mountainview since Andy was in fourth grade, he wanted nothing more than to leave, and the sooner, the better. Although she was sad, Danni understood when she had heard the news.

To hurt even more, the Bradleys decided to return to Daniel's native England. Nothing would ever be "right" for them in

Mountainview, and they wanted to give themselves, especially Jenny, a fresh start.

In a short time, Danni and Russell said goodbye to the Johnsons and the Bradleys, and they prayed that God would make something truly beautiful from something so painful.

5

Danni's arm hurt a lot but nothing like the pain in her soul. She was so lonely without Beth. Even though she adored Russell and always had, nothing seemed right. Russell reminded her of that night, and Danni reminded Russell of that night too. It was all so painful and confusing.

Danni graduated still wearing a cast, but at least it had been changed to a smaller one by that point. She was the valedictorian of her class. Russell was salutatorian. They both made touching speeches at their graduation ceremony and paused to reflect on how quickly life can change.

After their tassels had been flipped and caps thrown into the air with great joy, Danni felt a huge sense of relief. She ran to hug a few teachers. There had already been too many tears, and now was not the time for more.

Iris took Danni to a local fast-food restaurant. Although it wasn't fancy, at least Kurt and Ruby weren't there. They could attempt to eat in peace.

When she and Iris got home, Danni went to change clothes. Kurt slipped a thick envelope under her bedroom door. Over the last few years, he had taken to giving her an envelope full of money after he hit her or had "pouted" over some sin, real or imagined, that Kurt felt Danni had committed. "Oh, well, at least I can put this toward college expenses," she sighed as she put the money in her secret hiding place.

A few days later, Danni was thrilled when she got her cast

off. The doctor gave her a list of special exercises she had to do in order to regain the strength in that arm. "Oh, I will, Dr. Martin. I will!" Danni exclaimed, revealing one of the few real smiles she'd had since the accident. She hugged Dr. Martin, and then she and Iris hurried to Danni's Tempo.

Iris scowled as Danni started the car, and Danni wondered what she had done this time. She wisely decided not to say anything.

After they got home, Danni went to her room to change clothes. She'd recently taken up running and wanted to go for a run before it was too hot. North Carolina summers could be positively sweltering.

"Just what did you think you were doing back there?" Iris demanded, a lit cigarette bobbing up and down between her angry lips.

"Back where?" Danni asked, shrinking back from both Iris and the cigarette smoke that was assaulting her nostrils.

"You practically were all over Dr. Martin!" Iris accused, narrowing her eyes.

"I was not!" Danni shot back. "That's a disgusting thing to say."

"And you are a disgusting girl! An ungrateful brat!" Iris shot back. Before Danni realized it was coming, Iris slapped Danni so hard across the face that she caught her off guard and knocked her into her folding closet doors. The force of it propelled Danni through the doors so hard they splintered.

Danni landed in a heap, and it knocked the breath out of her. She had just gotten her cast removed, and Iris seemed bound and determined to break something else.

Without even waiting to see if Danni was okay, Iris spat out, "See what you made me do?" She spun on her heel and marched out, leaving a trail of stinky ashes on Danni's carpet, as Danni lay on the floor wondering how she would survive until college move-in day and why her mother, father, and grandmother all hated her so much. For about the millionth time, Danni wished it had been her and not Beth who had died in the accident.

Iris never apologized. She never acknowledged what she had done to Danni. Danni decided to keep her head down, her mouth shut, and decided to just bide her time.

The following weekend was "Orientation for Freshmen" weekend at Danni's new school. She was so excited. Parents were encouraged to attend too, and Kurt had agreed to go, much to everyone's surprise.

Following the tense two-and-a-half-hour ride, Danni signed in, dropped her things in a tiny dorm room on the fifth floor, and then hurried back to the lobby to find her parents. Iris looked nervous, and Kurt looked miserable. Danni felt like laughing, but she knew if she did, Kurt just might go ballistic.

Danni didn't want anything to mess up her weekend. She was more convinced, with each passing moment, that God was answering her fervent prayers for escape by blessing her with this scholarship. She wanted to honor Him and do something good with her life, and be as far away from Mountainview as possible.

Danni accompanied Iris and Kurt to the parents' dorm. Their room had bunk beds, which Danni secretly thought was hilarious. As Kurt's face reddened, Danni tamped down the urge to laugh. They deposited their small, faded overnight bags in the corner, and Danni left them to get settled.

She went to the language lab, with the help of her already dog-eared campus map, to take her French placement test. She sailed through it in no time.

Next, she walked three buildings over to take her math placement test. Math had never been her forte, so she really had to buckle down on it. By the time she was finished, her palms were so damp that she had to wipe them on her shorts. She prayed a silent prayer and thanked God for carrying her through that. Her stomach had cramped so bad that, at one point, she thought she was going to be sick.

After the math test was over, Danni made her way to McKnight Hall to hear a speaker discuss ways to succeed as a college freshman. She was amazed by the wide variety of students. There were people from all over the world, and Danni was looking forward to getting to know lots of different people.

Later that day, Danni met her advisor, Dr. Bob Gwent. Because she was a full scholarship student, she got to register early and see her placement scores before almost anyone else on campus. She had easily placed out of French and placed into Math 2. She thanked the Lord, sitting in Dr. Gwent's office that this was the "last stinking math class" she would ever have to take.

She looked at Dr. Gwent when she realized she'd prayed out loud and found him smiling too. Dr. Gwent endeared himself to Danni right then and there. He was a tiny, elfish man with bushy, dark hair and a thick mustache to match. With horn-rimmed glasses perched on the end of his nose, Dr. Gwent fit her image of a "nutty little professor."

However, Dr. Gwent was anything but nutty. He had her signed up for some interesting classes in no time. He gave her yet another packet of information to read. "We want you to meet the other teaching scholars after dinner. Some are arriving late, so that will give everyone a chance to get settled before we start the introductions," he explained.

Dr. Gwent told her where to meet them, shook her hand, and escorted her to the outer area of his office. "God bless you. We are glad to have you in our Charlotte family," he said warmly. With a smile and a wave, he disappeared into his office.

His words rang in Danni's ears. "Family." She had always wanted to belong but had never fit in anywhere. Maybe, just maybe, she would now have a chance to be accepted. Once again, a wave of grief and terror washed over Danni as she missed Beth so much that it was like her arm was missing.

Beth was family to her, more so than Iris, Kurt, and Ruby had ever been. Danni tearfully wondered what Beth would be doing if she had lived. "God, please get me through this," she prayed. "I'm so glad I don't have to do this alone." She smiled heavenward and felt peace as she continued on her way.

Later, Danni met Iris and Kurt for dinner in the large cafeteria. Kurt slinked around almost like he was afraid of something. It was amazing how subdued Kurt acted when he was out of the "safe element" of his home turf.

Iris broke into her thoughts. "Do you like it here?"

"Yes, I love it!" Danni said enthusiastically, drawing a blank stare from Iris and a dark scowl from Kurt.

Iris leaned in closely and whispered, "There are a lot of people here who are..different...from us." She raised her eyebrows and inclined her head toward some people, sitting a few tables away. They looked absolutely nothing like the Gradens, and Danni couldn't have cared less.

Iris whispered some ugly words to describe anyone who didn't look like them. "They're all alike, anyway. Disgusting," she said with a sniff.

Danni couldn't believe her ears. How in the world could these two even be a part of her gene pool? Scooting back her chair, Danni said, "Please excuse me. I need to go meet the other teaching scholars. I will see you at McKnight Hall tomorrow at eight a.m."

Danni hurried out of the cafeteria without a backward glance. Danni knew, from a young age, that there wasn't a lot of hope for any kind of relationship for her with either Kurt or Ruby. But, she had held out hope for so many years that someday, somehow, Iris would love her, really love her, the way a mom should love a daughter.

Finally, Danni realized that Iris just didn't have it in her. Whether it was Kurt and Ruby who had killed it in her, or Iris had done it to herself, it no longer mattered. What was done, was done. Danni forced the painful thoughts aside as she made her way to meet her fellow scholarship winners.

Dr. Gwent made his way to the podium and said, "Now don't be afraid. Everyone in this room has been vaccinated for rabies, so move in closer. Everyone gather around. We're here to get to know each other."

With that, the uncomfortable "ice" of being strangers was broken. Everyone laughed and moved in closer. Already, Danni could tell that Dr. Gwent was a special person. He spoke to them about the specifics of their scholarships, such as the exact requirements and expectations, privileges, etc.

The best thing Danni learned was that she didn't have to stay in the dorms. She was going to live in an apartment with two other honor students on the other side of campus. She would have her own bedroom and bathroom, and no one would bother her. It really was a dream come true! She wanted to cry!

Dr. Gwent then made his way down to the front row. He had each student stand up and introduce themselves. They laughed and talked and later moved to the reception area for punch and cookies. Danni liked the group and felt remarkably at ease in a relatively short period of time. No one said anything about her acne or punched her or made her feel bad.

One girl had a cane and walked with a slight limp. Nobody made fun of her. In fact, she was just one of the gang, and Danni was thrilled. For the first time in quite a while, she had hope for her future. She kept thinking about Jeremiah 29:11, which had always been one of her favorite verses.

6

At the end of the evening, Danni said goodnight to her new friends and walked back to the dorm. When she walked into her little room, she saw that she had still not been assigned a roommate for the night. So, she settled down and went to sleep, a smile playing at her lips, as she dreamed of the possibilities unfolding before her.

Several hours later, she was awakened by a loud thud. She sat up and grabbed her glasses. It was hard to see much of anything as she fumbled unsuccessfully for the light. "Who's there?" she asked, trying to sound all bad and tough.

"Ah, you can't see me in tha' dark, can ya' girl?" came a laughing, melodious reply. A second later, the blaring overhead light illuminated the body behind the voice.

A tall girl with dark skin, long dreadlocks, and a big smile eyeballed her. "Don't be afraid, now, I don't bite. I am LaMika LaRue from Louisiana. And who might you be?"

Danni shook her hand, liking her immediately. "I'm Danni from Mountianview, North Carolina."

"Ah, this Mountainview, that would be a 'hick town,' right?"

Danni laughed in spite of herself. "Yes, you can call it that," she admitted.

LaMika threw her head back and laughed, revealing a mouth full of perfect teeth. "Ah, you must tell me more about it, then."

And so, they sat up most of the night, sharing stories and getting to know each other. Danni was disappointed to learn that

LaMika would not be living in the scholars' apartments. "No, mon," she said. "We came back to my Papa's hometown in Louisiana from Jamaica right after he got sick. My own mama ran off right after I was born. Said she didn't want no 'screamin' brats,' so she jus' up and left. Papa left me some money, and Grandmama used it to raise me and send me to college. I have some real distant cousins in the area, so I thought I'd come here an' have myself an adventure. I didn't get a scholarship, so I'll be bunking down right here."

Danni smiled at the sound of LaMika's voice. It was an unusual blending of Jamaican and Louisiana drawl, and she just loved it. "What are you going to study?"

"Boys, as much as I can, and nursing, but not necessarily in that order," LaMika explained.

Finally, both girls fell asleep. Danni's annoying alarm clock woke them both at six-thirty. They laughed and giggled like old friends as they walked down to the dining hall for breakfast.

Before parting company, they exchanged contact information and promised to stay in touch in the fall. Danni quietly excused herself, regretting that she couldn't invite LaMika to eat with her because of her parents. It was one more reason she couldn't wait to leave Mountainview far behind in her rearview mirror.

Danni found Kurt and Iris already at a table. They ate quickly, saying little, and then made their way to the main auditorium to listen to one last speaker before leaving. The speaker wished them all well and droned on forever. Even Danni, who absolutely loved being there, was beginning to get bored.

After it was finally over, Iris and Kurt raced to the car, and both chain-smoked all the way home. Danni felt like a dog in the back seat as she rolled down the window and stuck her face out, desperately sucking in what little fresh air she could get into her lungs.

Iris said hatefully, "Well, I hope you enjoyed yourself, Miss Fancy Pants. We were miserable. We couldn't smoke, and when your father tried to, he set off an alarm, and a security guard came pounding on the door. He was a big, old black man, and we were afraid he'd whoop your daddy, so we had to stop. Then we had to take our cigarettes outside to sneak a puff. I've never seen anything like it." Iris was positively indignant.

Danni couldn't suppress a small giggle. It was so funny. She was just sorry she hadn't been there to witness it. Even though she wanted to gag because of the noxious fumes in the car, she was tickled by the thought of the security guard putting Kurt and Iris in their place.

When they arrived home, Danni was famished. She went to the kitchen and was surprised to find that Ruby had prepared lunch. She was pretending to sweep with a sickeningly sweet smile plastered on her face. As Danni sat down, Ruby pushed a big pile of trash on her.

Iris and Kurt, who had been in the living room, walked into the kitchen just in time to see Danni lunge at Ruby. Danni wanted to knock that broom right out of her hands.

As quick as a flash, Kurt slapped Danni now that he was back on his comfortable home territory. "Don't you ever disrespect my mother!" he bellowed.

"You are all crazy!" Danni yelled. She ran from the room with no one to defend her and no one to care. She escaped to her bedroom and locked the door. She flung herself onto her bed. After she nearly made herself sick from crying, Danni finally dried her eyes and went out to the front porch for some fresh air. She knew it was somewhat safe because Kurt had burned rubber out of the driveway almost as soon as Danni had retreated to her bedroom.

She took a few deep breaths and then wheeled around when someone grabbed her ponytail. "You little witch!" Iris screamed and flung Danni off the end of the porch. Danni landed in a crumpled heap in the grass. "If he gets into a wreck because of you, it will be all your fault. You are so stupid!" she screeched.

"I didn't make him drive," Danni said sadly, tears streaming down her face. "How is this my fault?" she asked pitifully, wondering for the thousandth time why they all hated her so much. Danni's lips were trembling so hard she could barely speak.

"It just is," was all Iris could manage to say. Her hands shook so violently she could barely hold and light the cigarette she had produced from somewhere. She lowered herself onto a cracked chair on the porch and puffed away, staring into space.

Fifteen minutes later, Kurt returned. He stormed into the house without speaking to anyone. He violently slapped Iris's hand away when she tried to touch his shoulder. Danni had pulled herself up by then, but her clothes were grass-stained. Nobody noticed. Nobody cared.

Once again, Beth's absence hit her like a ton of bricks. Even though Danni had never told Beth what was happening in her home, Danni always believed that Beth somehow knew anyway. And Danni knew she would never find a truer friend than Beth this side of heaven. She also knew she would miss her until the day she saw her again.

Danni showered, went to bed, and bright and early the next morning got a job at the local library. Although her parents had forbidden her from getting a job, she did it anyway. For the remainder of the summer, she stayed away from the house as much as possible. She loved working in the library and earning some money for her future.

7

The night before moving day was surreal for Danni. Hopefully she was closing the door on a very painful part of her life. Russell called her. His calls were few and far between now because it was just too awkward. As much as they cared about each other, it seemed that all they did was remind each other of what had once been and all that had been lost. They just wanted to move forward, somehow. They said a brief but sweet goodbye and knew that things could never be the same.

Andy had sent her a thoughtful card from California earlier in the week that made her cry. He was facing more surgery and rehab but was determined to make the best of things. He said that was how he wanted to honor Beth. Danni knew it was exactly what Beth would have wanted for each of them.

Although she only rarely heard from the Bradleys now that they were in England, they still contacted her from time to time. Their calls and cards were full of the same love they had always extended to Danni.

When she zipped up the last of her bags, Danni said a silent prayer for each of them. Their lives had all been forever changed in an instant, something none of them ever saw coming. But God was going to make their paths straight, somehow.

As she closed her bedroom door, Danni hoped her returns would be rare. The love and family she had so desperately wanted always eluded her here. She made sure she took the few possessions that meant something to her—mostly photos of her and

Beth, cards and letters, and two raggedy old stuffed animals.

Danni mumbled a forced good-bye to Ruby, and then she, Iris, and Kurt set off for the University of the Carolinas. Kurt drove his prized car, and Iris rode with Danni in her old clunker car. That way, Danni could have transportation around Charlotte. Neither Iris nor Danni said anything on the drive down. It was eerily quiet.

Danni thought about Beth again. Although Beth had not been as strong academically as Danni, she was a solid student and had always wanted to go to college with Danni. Andy had been in line for a football scholarship, but now Beth was gone. He was trying to walk without pain as he made his way through multiple surgeries and countless hours of physical therapy on the other side of the country.

In a last-minute surprise, Russell had announced he was going to spend at least a year in Africa, sharing Jesus and helping to bring clean water to people in desperate need. Nothing would ever be the same, but they were all doing their best to keep going.

After arriving at her new school, Danni worked with Kurt and Iris to unload her belongings. They did it in record time. Kurt was anxious to leave. Danni grinned as she remembered the burly security guard who had interrupted Kurt's smoking earlier in the summer.

"Well, we need to get going," Kurt announced. Without so much as a good-bye or even a hug, he turned on his heel and headed toward the parking lot, already fishing around in his pocket for a cigarette.

"I'm sure your father wants to get home and take a nap. All of this work today has made him tired," Iris said.

"What work?" Danni asked. "I don't have that much stuff, and you and I did most of the heavy lifting," Danni said.

"Don't sass me, young lady," Iris said, advancing on Danni.

Suddenly remembering where she was, Iris's entire demeanor changed. "After all, he is not quite as young as he used to be. He needs to take it easy. He works so hard for the family. It was nice of him to volunteer his time to come and move you in." Iris believed every word of her crazy fantasy. She really knew how to sell it.

Danni shook her head and said, "Okay, Mom. Take care." She moved in to hug Iris, but Iris just shrugged, mumbled a quick goodbye, and hurried after Kurt.

Danni stood watching them. They disappeared quickly and never turned around. Not even once. Danni smiled sadly and then went upstairs to unpack. After getting settled in, Danni prayed. "Dear God, please protect me and help me grow closer to You. Help me find my way," she said.

Afterward she went downstairs to the laundry room and washed everything she had brought with her, hoping to get the embarrassing stench of cigarette smoke out of her clothes. She ran everything through the wash cycle twice. Danni breathed in and out, slowly and carefully, reveling in the smell of her things finally smelling clean.

After getting everything moved into the dryers, Danni went back up to her new apartment and spun around the living room to celebrate her newfound freedom. Just then, the door flung open, and a whirlwind of activity sailed into the apartment.

With a strong Southern accent and an endearingly sweet smile, Sharon Bane introduced herself. "How do you do?" she asked.

"I'm just fine. It's so nice to meet you," Danni replied, smiling at her new roommate. Sharon was well-dressed in a red silk pair of shorts with a matching blouse. She had on a cute hat with tiny flowers on the brim and chunky, gold jewelry around both wrists, her neck, and several fingers. Sharon had a pretty face framed by springy, brown curls that danced around her head when she talked. She was about a foot shorter than Danni and the most animated person Danni had ever seen.

"Here, let me help you with that," Danni said as Sharon nearly collapsed under the weight of her designer luggage. Danni dragged the bags into the bedroom that was going to be Sharon's.

"Wow, they sure grow the gals tall where you're from," Sharon drawled.

Danni laughed. "I never thought about it that way before. I'm actually considered to be tall in my hometown," Danni explained. Danni liked Sharon already. She was funny and sweet.

A loud knock interrupted their talk. "Oh, that'll be my parents with the rest of my things," Sharon said sheepishly.

"The rest of your things?" Danni asked.

Sharon was serious. When she opened the door, a short, bald man came in, dragging three more large bags. He was followed by a tiny little sprite of a woman carrying two additional bags. They were obviously tired from all the work but were still smiling and cheerful.

"Hello, I'm Pat Bane," he said, extending a hand in Danni's direction. "And this is the love of my life, Darla. We are Sharon's personal moving crew."

As she was shaking hands with both Pat and Darla, Danni introduced herself. Danni liked them both immediately. As they moved things in and unpacked, Pat and Darla were friendly and chatty. Pat was an investment banker on Hilton Head Island in South Carolina. Darla was an at-home wife and mom and clearly relished it.

They talked a bit about Sharon's older brother, Paul, who was an up-and-coming artist in Paris. The Banes were obviously wealthy but incredibly unassuming, reminding Danni of Beth's family. It made her heart hurt a little to think about it.

Several hours later, Pat and Darla said a tearful goodbye to their daughter and left after hugging Danni and telling her what a "good girl" she was.

"Let me tell you about our other roomie," Sharon said as she and Danni enjoyed an exciting view of some cute guys playing a spirited game of volleyball outside their living room window. The apartment was fully and tastefully furnished in a modern, chic style, and it was beyond anything Danni could have ever hoped for.

"Do you know her already?" Danni asked.

"Yeah, I do," Sharon answered. "You'll like her. Her name is Jana Sharpe, and she's a teaching scholar just like you. She's not wealthy, but her parents are great. They spoil their only child as much as they can. Jana works hard, and she keeps to herself while she's studying. She takes school seriously."

Danni nodded reflectively. Before she could reply, someone knocked on the door. Sharon nearly tripped over herself to answer it.

A tall, lanky guy with dark, fuzzy hair strolled in. He hugged Sharon tightly. "Oh, Dan, I'm so glad you made it!" Sharon grinned from ear to ear.

Sharon introduced Dan Martin as "the man she was going to marry." They both smiled and seemed happy together. Danni learned that Dan had recently graduated and was working for an advertising agency downtown. From the sound of things, he was a real go-getter.

Dan already had some money saved so he and Sharon could get married as soon as she finished her accounting degree, which should be in about two more years.

Sharon proudly said that her parents and brother, Paul, all loved Dan and were one hundred percent in support of them, as long as they waited to marry until Sharon finished her degree, which sounded perfectly reasonable to Danni.

Finally, Jana arrived with her parents, Will and Wanda, in tow. They were all hot, sweaty, and tired. They were older than Danni would have expected, with gray hair and pleasant faces. Danni rushed to get some water to refresh them.

Jana was of medium height with light brown, shoulder-length hair. She was pretty and stylish without being overly fussy with her clothes and makeup, and Danni immediately liked her.

With thanks uttered and introductions made, they sat down in the living room, and Jana explained the story. She said, "Mom and Dad and I actually got started down on time, but the car choked and belched and then died. It took almost four hours for someone to tow it and get Big Beula running again." Jana had everyone in stitches in no time.

They all teamed up and got Jana's things moved in and set up in record time. It was obvious that she was a very organized girl. Jana hugged her parents tightly, and they left quickly, lest they have more trouble out of Big Beula on the way back home.

Jana turned to Danni and said, "So, Sharon tells me that you are a teaching scholar too. As it turns out, I got a letter from Dr. Gwent last week saying that I have been selected to be your mentor. Pretty clever, huh?" she asked with a grin.

"That's great!" Danni beamed, glad to have another friend who seemed eager to help. "I met Dr. Gwent at orientation back in June, and he seemed terrific."

"He is," Jana agreed. "He has rearranged my schedule so many times that I think I am the reason he has so much gray hair!" Jana laughed.

Half an hour later, Dr. Gwent dropped by to see Jana and Danni. "Are you two settling in okay?" he asked.

They both laughed about how much fun they were having.

"She's better than the other ten you sent me," Jana said with a straight face.

"Shhh. You promised not to tell," Dr. Gwent replied, going along with the joke. He then turned to Danni and said, "It can all be a bit overwhelming at first. Please don't hesitate to call me if you need anything." He saluted the ladies and then left.

"I can't believe how nice he is," Danni said, still amazed.

"Well, he is. I heard from a senior last year that he has always been a super-nice guy. His only child, a son, committed suicide about five years ago. Somehow, he went off track and got into drugs and had a lot of trouble with the law. Dr. Gwent and his wife did everything they could do to help, but they just couldn't reach him in time. After his son died, Dr. Gwent made it like a personal crusade to take extra-good care of his students. I guess he doesn't want to ever see anything like that happen to any of us," Jana stated.

"That must have been terrible," Danni said, thinking of losing Beth. She couldn't even imagine losing her own child. She thought about how it must have been a nightmare for Dr. Gwent and his wife.

The conversation then turned to a much lighter note. Dan had to leave, and Sharon walked over to the other two and said, "I have been misled. Nobody told me I would have to room with Barbie." She made an exaggerated ugly face, and the others laughed.

"Yeah!" Jana added. "We are never going to have a moment's peace around here. I think we'll just slide a paper bag over Danni's head and be done with it."

Danni was surprised at her new friends' comments. No one had ever said anything like that to her before except Russell and Beth. She had always thought they did it out of a sense of obligation to her since they were such close friends. Her skin had begun clearing up dramatically the closer it got to her college move-in date. "Thank you, but I don't really think that will be a problem," she said.

"Now don't you dare go telling me that you don't have guys chasing you 24/7 back home!" Jana accused, playfully wagging a finger at Danni.

"Not even close," Danni said. "In addition to 'Gangly Giant,' they've called me some really clever names over the years," Danni said sadly,

"Girl, those punks were just threatened by you. That's all over now. Welcome to some fine honeys!" Jana said, and Sharon nodded her head in agreement. Jana then added, "You and I are going to meet ourselves some quality fellas. Sharon is practically married already, so she doesn't count."

Sharon stuck her tongue out at Jana. "Yeah, but that doesn't mean I can't look!"

The two teachers-to-be collapsed onto the sofa in a fit of laughter. And so, the tone in apartment 307 was set. The girls easily fell into a comfortable routine and got along famously, often staying up way too late, giggling and talking.

8

That Sunday, Danni set off in search of a church. She had researched several churches online and visited the one she thought was the best fit. It was a sweet church within walking distance from campus. She liked it right away and was happy to learn they had an on-campus Bible study every Thursday night. She definitely wanted to check that out too.

Danni had invited Sharon and Jana to accompany her. Both girls were somewhat interested but didn't want to get up early the day before classes started. Danni had already figured out that neither girl had committed themselves to Jesus, so she had added them to her daily prayer list. "We'll have to see about that," she said as she prayed and smiled heavenward. Danni already liked her roommates far too much to not try to tell them about Jesus.

Dan quickly became a fixture around apartment 307, yet somehow managed to never pester anyone. He was more like a big, goofy brother to Jana and Danni. He was also handy, so anytime they had a minor repair, it was usually easier and faster to get Dan to take a look instead of waiting on the maintenance department to get to it. Dan reminded Danni of Russell, which was a great comfort to her. Jana also liked Dan a lot. She loved arguing with him about politics and world affairs. If he disagreed with her, she just pummeled him with a pillow. Sharon thought it was all great fun and egged them both on.

For the tenth time since school started, Dan made himself comfortable on the living room sofa as he looked squarely at

Danni. "I'm telling you, he's perfect for you. Just meet him once, tell me you are not interested in him, and that will be that. I promise." Dan held up his hand and nodded solemnly.

"Dan, I'm sorry, but nobody is as wonderful as this Robert what's-his-name." She put down her history book and gave him a dark look, pretending to be angry with him.

Sharon interrupted, "Danni, he is so sweet it's positively sickening. He's tall, handsome, and has his own business. He'll be stopping by the day before we leave for Thanksgiving break. He will be on his way home to New Jersey from a business trip and has a layover between his flights. He wanted to stop by and see us."

"Gee, how wonderful," Danni said dramatically, rolling her eyes. "If I'm here, I guess it won't kill me to greet him. But if you embarrass me, I promise I will tie you up in the middle of the courtyard and leave you there."

Danni stuck out her tongue, and Dan threw a decorative pillow at her. Sharon laughed as Jana stuck her head out of her room and threatened everyone if they couldn't keep quiet. She had a big math test the next day, and she declared that she would personally do great bodily harm to the next person who made a peep.

The silence lasted all of four seconds before the foursome burst into laughter. Each one blamed the other for the noise, but it didn't matter, anyway. Laughter was common in the apartment.

The only drawback to Danni's newfound existence was Iris. She called her every single day. She never wanted or needed anything important. She just wanted to hang onto Danni, even if only over the telephone. Danni was beginning to get embarrassed by it. "Mom, you really don't have to call me every day. Why don't we talk once or twice a week?" she suggested.

Her request was met with silence. It took a few moments before Iris spoke again. "Well, everyone was right. They told me you'd get yourself down to that fancy school, with your fancy scholarship, and you'd forget about us. You think you're too good for us now!" Iris peppered Danni's ears with a few obscenities, then hung up abruptly.

Danni had never had Iris hang up on her before, which momentarily stunned her. She sat there looking at the phone for long moments. She didn't quite know what to do or even how to feel. Finally she got out her Bible and read Psalm 91. She felt like she needed all the protection she could get, and she knew God would provide it.

Danni just couldn't figure Iris out. She'd been there all those years, just begging for Iris to notice her and pay attention to her. But Danni felt like all she ever was to Iris was a bother. Kurt and Ruby never called or wrote to Danni, but she didn't care. She expected that as long as she didn't bother them, they wouldn't bother her.

Classes were easy for Danni and Jana. They even had two literature classes together, which they greatly enjoyed. On the other hand, Sharon didn't have their aptitude for learning unless it involved Dan. He even tried to give her more time and space to devote to her studies, but it did little good. Sharon hit the books a bit harder only when Pat and Darla threatened to make her return home.

Danni had the pleasure of running into LaMika LaRue several times around campus. The two were always glad to see each other. LaMika hugged Danni and said, "How ya been doin', mon? Ya lookin' great."

"Thanks. You do too," Danni replied. Danni had to grin. LaMika was quite a character. Her dreadlocks had grown even longer, and she now had her nose pierced. Danni knew Iris would have had a snit fit if she knew that Danni and LaMika were friends. They talked for a bit, and then LaMika said, "I've gotta run, mon. But why dontcha come to me party on Saturday night? It's gonna be some big fun!"

Danni almost declined but changed her mind. "Well, I guess I can stop by. I have some things to do on Saturday, but I can come by afterward."

"Great, mon. I'll see you then!" LaMika said and gave Danni all the details. With a big smile and a wave, she took off in the opposite direction from where Danni was headed.

On Saturdays, Danni was pretty much on her own. Jana either locked herself in her room or camped in the library, depending on how much school work she had to do. After she completed all of her work, she either treated herself to a milkshake or a movie and went to bed early, unless she had plans to hang out with her roomies.

Sharon flew through her homework as fast as possible to spend time with Dan. Her grades had steadily improved, but it was a constant battle for her.

Danni secured a job working at the on-campus bookstore and also volunteered at the Charlotte Downtown Mission. She had overheard some kids talking in the bookstore check-out line about what a shame it was about all of the food that got thrown away at the campus dining hall.

After doing some investigating, Danni learned it was true. She connected the head of the campus dining services with the head of the Charlotte Downtown Mission. It took some sweet-talking and lots of paperwork, but Danni was able to help put together an agreement that the school would donate leftover food to help feed the people at the mission. Danni loaded up her battered old car several times a week and hauled food to the mission. She had recruited five other people to help her. Three of them were Jana, Sharon, and Dan.

It happened to be a short workday at the bookstore. Danni

finished up and then hurried to the back entrance of the dining hall. She loaded up five gigantic containers of food and hurried over to the mission. She wanted to finish in time to get all spiffed up for LaMika's party that night. No matter what, LaMika was a lot of fun, and Danni was glad to know her. She was really looking forward to the get-together.

When Danni pulled up to the Charlotte Downtown Mission, she was met by her usual helper, Jake. Jake was a huge guy. Danni thought he had to be close to seven feet tall. He had really dark skin and one brown eye and one blue eye. His hair was in the most fluffy Afro Danni had ever seen.

Jake had shared his story with Danni as they worked side-by-side many times each week. He was a veteran who had severe PTSD after returning home from three back-to-back tours of duty. He had become an alcoholic and lost his wife and daughter. His ex-wife had remarried, and she, their daughter, and her new husband had been killed in a plane crash not long after his ex-wife remarried. That's when Jake had hit rock bottom. He ended up at the mission, and the director introduced him to Jesus shortly afterward.

It was hard, but Jake had made his way back. He had been working full-time at the mission for several years when Danni first started making her food deliveries. She always enjoyed talking with him. He could quote the Bible like no one Danni had ever met, but what really impressed her was how Jake made the Bible come alive when he talked. He was able to understand and apply the meaning of Scripture to real life. It made her want to do that too.

"Hey there, Jake. How are you today?" Danni asked with a big smile.

"Oh, I'm just fine, little lady. How are you?"

"I'm great now," Danni beamed. She loved helping at the mission. Whenever time allowed, she would not only deliver the food, she would also stay and help serve it. Since it was a Christian-run mission, she was encouraged to share Jesus with the people who came in. With Jake's guidance, she felt brave enough to pray with people at the mission. At first, she was a bit nervous and uncomfortable, but with Jake's guidance and her re-dedication to her Bible study and prayer life, she grew more and more confident in sharing her faith in lots of ways. It made Danni's heart sing.

Just before she left for the day, Danni saw the same young girl she'd seen many times. She had to be close to Danni's age. She said her name was Carla, but Danni didn't think that was her real name. Many of the people at the mission didn't give their real names. Nobody cared; they just wanted to help.

"Hi, Carla,"‘ Danni said as she put a hand on the girl's bony shoulder. Carla jumped about a foot. "Oh, I'm so sorry. I didn't mean to startle you," Danni said, immediately regretting touching her.

"It's...it's okay," Carla said weakly. Her hair was stringy and hung halfway down her back, and her skin was so pale you could almost see her veins. Her blue eyes looked haunted, almost vacant. Danni could only imagine what the poor girl had been through in her young life. It made Danni's heart feel heavy to see Carla, and she constantly had to fight back waves of tears.

"Would you like something to eat? We've got some really great things today," Danni said with a smile.

Carla's face lit up at the mention of food. "Yes, I'm starving," she said.

Danni thought she literally was starving. Despite the fairly warm weather, Carla had on a thick, over-sized sweater, a long, battered-looking skirt, and worn-out combat boots. All of it was too big for her.

Danni served up a plate of spaghetti and meatballs, bread, and a small salad. She gladly agreed when Carla asked her to sit with her while she ate. "So, how is Harvey?" Danni asked as Carla dug into the food.

For a moment, Carla's face clouded over. "He's...he's..." Carla had run away from her abusive home in rural Arkansas to be with Harvey in the hope of a better life. They wound up in Charlotte while Harvey supposedly looked for work. Carla worked when she could.

Danni couldn't prove it, but she knew in her heart that Harvey was abusing Carla. She knew the signs all too well. She'd become an expert herself at hiding the abuse and making up all kinds of stories and excuses in the name of protection. She identified so much with Carla, more than Carla could possibly understand.

After Carla gratefully finished her meal, she let Danni pray with her before they said goodbye.

Danni thought about Carla on the drive back to campus. She was so grateful that God had given her a way out of Mountainview with her scholarship. She prayed often that He would deliver Carla away from Harvey's abusive hands.

Danni was grateful that she had been able to open a bank account of her own. Kurt and Iris would never have allowed her to do that before. She deposited all of the money that Kurt and Ruby had given her as bribes over the years, and each time she got her bookstore paycheck, she added as much as she could to her account. It all helped her feel independent for the first time in her life. And for that, she was beyond grateful. She just wanted the same thing for Carla and was determined to help her somehow.

9

Danni arrived back at the apartment in time to shower and get ready for the party at LaMika's. After she showered and dried her strawberry blond hair, which now hung over halfway down her back, Danni brushed it into a sleek, high ponytail. Her face had taken on a new definition—she had a heart-shaped face, killer high cheekbones, huge green eyes, and a rosebud mouth that loved to smile.

She was beautiful enough to stop traffic, but her old fears and insecurities kept her from seeing what those around her saw. She saw the acne-laden kid with desert-dry skin who was as tall and gangly as a giraffe. She had to fight to keep from hearing and listening to the hate-laced voices of Iris, Kurt, and Ruby echoing inside her head.

Danni put on a bit of makeup and then slipped into a pair of white jeans and a red silk blouse. She walked over to Scott Hall and headed to the elevator. When the elevator stopped on the fifth floor, the music was rocking.

When she rounded the corner to the common area near LaMika's room, Danni laughed to see LaMika directing a limbo contest with about fifteen eager contestants. She was holding a bright neon-green broom as people fell under it, left and right.

As soon as she saw Danni, LaMika almost dropped the broom. She quickly handed the broom off to someone else and yelled, "Hey, mon, come on over. I've got somebody for ya to meet."

Danni made her way over to where her friend stood, careful not to mess up the limbo contestants' concentration. When she got there, she looked into the eyes of a truly beautiful man. He absolutely took her breath away. His eyes were a brilliant blue, reminding her of a summer sky in the middle of June. He was tall and lanky with nicely defined muscles under his dark green shirt. His long legs were handsomely encased in a pair of designer jeans. He looked like an ad campaign come to life. Danni's mouth suddenly went dry.

"Danni, from North Carolina, I want you to meet me personal friend, Mr. Jeff Kingston, from parts unknown," LaMika said.

"It's a pleasure to meet you, Danni," Jeff said with a smile, revealing perfect white teeth.

"It's nice to meet you, too," Danni said. She felt like there was a huge wad of cotton in her mouth. Or perhaps she had swallowed her tongue. Danni loved to talk and was normally never at a loss for words. But this time, she felt completely bowled over. She remembered Sharon's quote about "a man of beauty was a joy forever," and it surely applied to this fine fella. He was positively exquisite.

From that moment on, Danni and Jeff spent the entire time at the party deep in conversation. She learned that he was an only child of doting parents. They had traveled all over the world due to his father's job in communications. He'd lived in the area once as a young boy and returned because it was one of his favorite places in the world.

Jeff was double majoring in English and psychology because he said he wanted to be a writer and also be able to understand the kind of warped mind it takes to be successful at it. Jeff said, "God is good, and He orders our steps the way they should be."

"So you're a Christian too?" Danni asked.

"Yes, I am. I can't imagine where my life would be if I weren't," he said honestly. "What about you?"

"I sure am," Danni said, her heart soaring. "And I couldn't agree with you more." Danni was entranced by Jeff. And he was equally smitten by her. They couldn't stop smiling at each other, and from her observation point, LaMika mentally high-fived herself. She knew, just absolutely knew, that they would like each other, and by the looks of things, she was right.

At the end of the successful party, Jeff said, "May I give you a lift? My car is parked just outside. I don't like the idea of you walking home alone."

Danni was touched by his concern. "Sure, that would be great."

They took the elevator back down, and he escorted her to his black Porsche. Jeff opened her door and helped her in before sliding behind the wheel.

"This is a beautiful car," Danni said.

"Thank you. It was a present from Mom and Dad."

"For your birthday?" Danni inquired. She was eager to know all about him.

"No, it was for getting a scholarship, kind of a celebratory gift," he explained a bit sheepishly.

"Congratulations!" Danni exclaimed. "Which one?"

"The Chandra E. Knowles Scholarship," he said as they pulled into Danni's parking lot.

"That's the most prestigious writing scholarship in the whole country!" Danni exclaimed. "That is awesome! You must be a genius." She clapped her hands in delight.

"I don't know about that," Jeff said. He was pleased that she didn't hold it against him. Success bred a lot of funny emotions in people, especially jealousy. Danni didn't appear to have one jealous bone in her body, which pleased Jeff immensely. Even though he was still in college, he had almost finished his first novel, and he wanted to be a successful writer. He was committed to his craft.

Once they parked, Jeff asked, "May I walk you to your door?"

"You certainly may," she replied with a smile.

When they reached the entrance to her building, Jeff said, "I had a wonderful time tonight. May I call you tomorrow?"

"Yes, I'd like that," Danni smiled. She found a scrap of paper and a pen in her bag and wrote down her number.

Danni sighed happily and practically floated on air as she quietly entered the apartment. Jana and Sharon had long since gone to sleep. Danni thanked God for nudging her to attend the party. She prayed for LaMika and Jeff and asked God to help her not get her heart too involved too soon. She really liked him already and wanted to make sure she didn't get ahead of what God had planned.

She also prayed for Jake at the mission and Carla. She had to force herself to pray for Carla's boyfriend, Harvey, but she did. Finally she asked God to bless Sharon, Dan, Jana, and her family back home too. By the time she'd completed her prayer list, Danni fell asleep with a big smile and had lovely dreams. She slept so well that she almost missed church the next morning.

Just as she was walking back into the apartment after church, she saw a hastily scribbled note from Sharon. It said she and Dan were shopping and that Jana was at the library again. The phone began ringing just as Danni put up her purse.

"Hi, beautiful," Jeff greeted her.

"How did you know it was me?" Danni asked, unable to keep the smile out of her voice.

"You have the most charming Southern accent I've ever heard, and I do believe I could pick it out anywhere, anytime," Jeff replied.

Danni laughed, "You sure are something."

"I'm going to take that as a compliment of the highest order."

"You should."

"Would you care to join me for a picnic?" he asked.

"I'd love to. I just got home from church. Give me ten minutes to change, and I can be ready," Danni said.

"Sounds great. See you in a bit," Jeff replied.

Danni hung up and raced to her room. She found a cute pair of jeans and a soft purple sweater. It was a trendy yet lady-like outfit. She scurried out the door and had to remind herself to take a deep breath and just relax and slow down.

When she reached the main entrance of the apartment building, he was waiting just outside, smiling and armed with Sterling roses, her favorite.

"These are so beautiful," Danni said, touched that he'd paid that much attention to her the night before.

"And so are you," he smiled. He offered her his arm as they made their way to his Porsche. He helped her inside, and then they were off.

"Where, exactly, are we going?" Danni asked.

"Ah, my dear. Good things come to those who wait," Jeff replied with a grin.

They fell into a comfortable silence as Jeff expertly maneuvered the sleek car onto the highway. The day was absolutely stunning. There wasn't a cloud in the sky, and the weather was unusually warm for that time of the year.

Half an hour later, Jeff took the exit to Lake Norman. They drove for a few more minutes before he rolled down a long, winding driveway that reached a dead-end right on the water. Towering trees that must have been there for hundreds of years lined both sides of the land, and the white gravel crunched softly under the car as Jeff purred to a stop.

"This is gorgeous!" Danni exclaimed excitedly as she caught sight of the beautiful, two-story Tudor-style home off to one side. It reminded her faintly of Beth's parents' house. Even the entrance was similar. The lovely, well-manicured lawn and the brightly colored flowers reminded her of rare happy days from long ago. She felt tears catch in her throat. She almost expected Beth to come stepping out from behind a tree to tell her that it had all been some kind of mistake and that she was alive and well.

Not wanting Jeff to see her that way, Danni quickly jumped out of the car without waiting for Jeff to get the door. She walked toward the lake and stopped by the water's edge to gaze out at the stunning horizon.

Sensing all was not well, Jeff followed her quietly. "What's wrong, Danni?" Concern showed in his eyes as he gently turned her to face him. His powerful arms were both strong and tender at the same time.

"I don't...I...can't..." Danni trailed off, not wanting to face it but knowing she had to.

"Whatever it is, you can trust me. I know I just met you, Danni, but I already know you're special. I also know that you have been in pain for a long time. I can feel it. You need somebody to care, and I would like to be that person." He uttered the words softly in her ear, just barely above a whisper, but the meaning left no confusion in Danni's mind or her heart. Jeff gently took Danni's hand in his and quietly led her to a fallen tree, and they sat down on it, side-by-side.

The unshed tears and years of pent-up emotions swirled within her, and Danni could no longer contain any of them. She cried as she told him the ugly secrets of her family—the years of beatings and cruelty and the absolute terror she felt daily in the Graden family.

"There are just so many questions I have, so many things I

don't understand," Danni sobbed. "I don't know why they hate me so much. And to top it off, my mom acts like she hates me about ninety-nine percent of the time, and then once-in-a-great-while, she will fool me into thinking she actually cares about me. Like an idiot, I fall for it every time." Her tears became sobs, wracking her entire body.

Jeff sat there, stunned. He came from such a warm and loving family that it was difficult to even fathom the hurt and heartbreak Danni had suffered for so long. "Danni, I am so sorry." He put an arm around her shoulders and felt that she was still shaking. He handed her a handkerchief, which she gratefully accepted.

Once she had somewhat regained her composure, Danni said, "For the life of me, I can't understand why, but I still love my mom. At least part of me does. I still pray that she will leave those two nuts and just get out of there, but I don't think it will happen. I think she just gave up on life a long time ago, and now she is just an angry shell of her former self. "

"Danni, I want you to know that I will do anything to help you. Thank you for sharing this with me," Jeff said calmly, while a storm was raging inside. He silently prayed for calmness. He was nearly overcome by the horror of what Danni had been through.

"I've never shared this with anyone," Danni said sadly. Danni told him then about Beth and the accident, further breaking Jeff's heart and making him feel even more honored that she wanted to confide in him.

Jeff offered to pray with Danni, which couldn't have come at a better moment. "Dear Lord, thank You that we can pray about anything and You will hear us. Thank You for Danni. Thank You for making her strong. Lord, I can't imagine the hurt she has suffered, but You can. You were with her, and You will bring her through this. Please protect her and heal her and help her give her hurt to You. Thank You for bringing us into each other's lives. In the name of Jesus, Amen." Jeff hugged Danni, and she took his hand when he offered it. He helped her up, and they both dusted off after sitting on the fallen log.

Life had changed dramatically for both of them in the last twenty-four hours. They felt it. No words were needed; they both just knew.

Attempting to lighten the mood, Jeff said, "Well, I kicked the man and woman who lived here out and told them I was bringing a beautiful damsel here, just so I could try to impress her," he said dramatically, making Danni giggle in spite of herself.

As they made their way to the house, Jeff produced a key, and they went inside. It was just as impressive on the inside as on the outside. The downstairs rooms were done in alternating light blue and gray silks, and the floors were marble. Perfectly appointed antique furniture adorned each room. The formal dining room had two mirrored walls that made the room seem to stretch endlessly before them. "May I show you the upstairs?" he asked.

"Sure," Danni replied. She was even more impressed with the upstairs. Each bedroom was exquisitely decorated in a beautiful floral print and had its own private bath done in coordinating colors.

The master bedroom took her breath away. It was pale green and white with a huge fireplace. Windows lined one entire side of the bedroom, allowing the impressive scenery of the lake to capture her eye.

"What were you thinking just then, pretty lady?"

"I think I'm just really glad to be here," she replied quietly. A small smile played on her lips.

"Me too," Jeff said. "Now, how about some lunch by the lake?" he asked.

Jeff led her outside to a beautiful picnic-style table, and then he brought the picnic hamper over from his car. Jeff had prepared a feast of fresh fruit, cheese, bread, Caesar salad, and his favorite mineral water. It was truly a picture-perfect day.

Jeff and Danni moved on to lighter subjects after the heaviness of Danni's earlier revelation. They soon laughed and talked like old friends. Each thought the other was definitely an old soul, and it suited them both well. It was hard to believe they had only known each other for such a short time.

"Okay, how do you know the owners of this awesome place?"

"My parents own it. I actually live here," Jeff said, a bit sheepishly. He knew he was blessed, and he was always conscious of not rubbing it in on others. He especially didn't want to make Danni feel bad about anything.

After they finished their feast, Jeff insisted on cleaning up. He then rolled up his perfectly pressed jeans and ditched his Gucci loafers. "Let's check out the water temperature," he suggested.

"If you insist," Danni said. She quickly took off her shoes and socks and followed Jeff's lead. They chased each other through the edge of the water and were soon laughing and splashing each other. They were pleased to discover the water was warmer than they'd first thought it would be.

After a while, Jeff said he had some work to do, so she suggested they begin making their way back to reality.

They journeyed back to Danni's apartment, enjoying a comfortable silence, each lost in their own thoughts. Jeff was still struggling to understand why Danni had suffered so much and was amazed by how together she was. He knew he'd have to spend a lot of time in prayer later to deal with the anger he was feeling toward Danni's family.

"Will you please come up and meet my roommates?" Danni asked as they pulled into the parking lot.

"For you, anything," Jeff said, smiling.

Danni grabbed her bag, and they headed inside. She signed him in at the front desk, and they rode the elevator up to the third floor. Danni laughed when she opened the door because Jana, Dan, and Sharon were having one of their classic discussions. This time it was about a radical political group in Guatemala. Just in time, Danni yelled, "Duck!" so she and Jeff could avoid getting smacked over the head by a flying pillow.

"I see nothing changes when I step out of the room for a while," Danni said, shaking her head at her mischievous friends.

"Hi, Mom!" all three chorused in unison.

"Very funny, guys," Danni retorted. "If you all can behave yourselves, I want you to meet a friend of mine. Jeff Kingston, I would like you to meet Jana, Dan, and Sharon."

Dan quickly shook hands with Jeff, and Jana and Sharon greeted him warmly. The girls were obviously impressed by the newcomer. In a few short minutes, the five of them were involved in another discussion, this one involving a trade agreement with China. Jeff was charming, witty, and hilarious. In no time flat, the others had clearly accepted Jeff, which thrilled Danni.

Before they knew it, it was almost ten-thirty. Jeff said he had work waiting for him, and he had to go. Danni walked him downstairs and hugged him tightly at the front entrance. "Thank you for everything," she whispered.

"You're welcome. This is just the beginning," he replied. He really wanted to kiss her, but he wanted to do things right, so he kept telling himself to just be cool.

10

By the time Danni got back upstairs, Sharon was on her way back up from walking Dan out. Danni absently noticed several sticky notes on their group message board near the inside of the apartment's front door. Apparently Iris had already called three times that night.

Jana literally pounced on Danni before she had a chance to even think about calling Iris. "Out with it!" she demanded. "Where did you find that hunky specimen of a man? Does he have a brother?'

Danni laughed. "I met him at LaMika's party. She and Jeff are friends, and she thought we might like each other, so she introduced us."

"He was great!" Sharon added her opinion to the conversation. "Remember, 'a man of beauty is a joy forever,'" Sharon sang and twirled around the room. "That phrase was custom-made for Mr. Jeff Kingston!"

"Danni, just be careful. I don't want to see you get hurt," Jana said. "I can tell you really like him." Jana put her arm around Danni's shoulders and hugged her. "I have to worry about someone. Sharon stays so busy chasing after Dan that I don't see her quite enough to worry about her."

Danni went to sleep easily, and for the first time in a long time, only had one nightmare. Her sleep usually was peppered with bad dreams, so this was quite a breakthrough for her. She completely forgot about calling Iris until the next day. She knew it inevitably would be an ugly conversation, but Danni did her best to put it out of her mind.

Late that afternoon, Jeff called and asked Danni to dinner. She happily accepted and changed into a pretty purple dress. Sharon styled Danni's hair into a beautiful, intricate braid, and she was all ready to go when Jeff arrived. He took her to L'Etienne, a trendy French restaurant in the uptown district. Jeff surprised her with a carriage ride after dinner.

"Danni, I know this is fast, but I am falling in love with you," he said as he took her hand.

Taken aback, Danni didn't say anything for a long time. Finally, she replied, "I love you too." Danni sighed and laid her head on his shoulder.

After the carriage ride, they happily held hands and strolled through Queen's Park on the way back to Jeff's car. "Danni, please fly back to Chicago with me for Thanksgiving. I know it's short notice, but I don't want to be away from you." His beautiful blue eyes pleaded with her.

"Ugh. No fair. How can I resist you?" Danni asked. "The only problem is my mom. She will have a fit and really make my life miserable if she doesn't meet you first. Look, I know it's a lot to ask, considering what I've shared with you, but will you meet my parents for dinner and let them see that you don't have a pitchfork and horns?"

Jeff stopped and faced Danni. "I would love to say I'm excited about it, but I can't. I don't want to lie to you, but yes, I will be glad to meet your parents."

Danni hugged him. "It's complicated, I know. Thank you for doing this." Just then, Danni's brain registered how soon Thanksgiving was. "Wait a minute! Thanksgiving is next week! I don't have a plane ticket, and what will I wear, and—"

Jeff cut her off. "Hit the brakes. First thing's first. I will get you the ticket. It's my gift to you since I invited you. What you wear is up to you. It'll be cold, so a bathing suit is probably not the best idea, although I am certain the view would be great!"

"Will your parents mind?" Danni asked worriedly. She looked so earnest that it made Jeff love her even more.

"I called them this morning and asked. My mom has been praying for some time that I would meet a 'nice friend' as she put it. She cheered so loudly that I think my hearing is going to be permanently rattled in my right ear," Jeff explained. "She and my dad will love you."

And so it was settled. Danni wanted to hurry back to the apartment so she could begin planning her wardrobe. But she also knew she had to make the dreaded phone call to Iris. When she finally dialed the number, Iris answered on the first ring. Danni quickly told her about meeting Jeff and his invitation to Chicago.

"You mean you would leave us all alone here on Thanksgiving, just so you can spend the holiday with a complete stranger?" Iris hissed. She was livid, and Danni mentally kicked herself for even caring. Iris pretended to cry, sniffing loudly into the phone.

Danni wasn't fooled by her crocodile tears. "Believe it or not, Mom, I am not doing this to hurt you. I love Jeff, and he loves me. It's not about you."

"Clearly," Iris snorted.

Danni asked her again about meeting for dinner.

"Well, I guess my own daughter isn't giving me much of a choice," she spat.

"Mom, I want to include you. Please don't make this hard. Enjoy it. Be happy for me, please," Danni pleaded.

"There is no enjoyment in this life for me," Iris whined. "Give me the name of the restaurant and time, and your father and I will be there."

Danni gave her the details for the restaurant Jeff had suggested, and then she rattled on about what she was going to wear in an effort to make small talk.

"Don't tell me this is a fancy restaurant," Iris said. "You know how your father feels about those types of places."

"Mom, his idea of 'fancy' is Burger King or McDonald's. This is a nice restaurant, but he's a big boy. Surely he can make it through one evening. I have never asked for a lot, and I don't think this should be a big deal now," Danni said, wondering where the courage to stand up for herself came from. She was shaking and had to fight to keep the anxiety out of her voice, as her stomach felt like it was turning somersaults.

"Fine," Iris conceded coolly. "We'll see you on Friday night." With that, Iris hung up.

As Danni prayed before bed and did her best to focus on the positive, Iris was chain-smoking and cursing back in Mountainview. She was so angry her hand shook as she dialed the number she knew so well. Tom Markori was sleazy, for sure, but he could dig up dirt on just about anyone. Unbeknownst to anyone else, Iris had employed his services a number of times over the years to check on Kurt's activities. She was going to get rid of this pesky Jeff Kingston. Do-gooder Danni wouldn't want anything to do with him once Iris got the dirt on him.

But by Friday, Iris was practically livid. As hard as he tried, Tom had failed her this time. There simply was no dirt to be found on Jeff or his family. That made Iris want to explode. How was it fair for Danni to be happy when she was miserable? What made Danni more deserving of happiness than she was?

"Listen, Iris," Tom Markori said. "This Jeff guy is great. He is exactly the kind of guy every mother should want her daughter to find. They are a solid, Christian family. Made their money—and they have plenty of it—through hard work and smarts. Just accept it and be happy for your daughter."

Iris cut her eyes toward her husband sprawled out lazily on the floor in front of the television, snoring loudly. A sharp pang of jealousy cut her to her core. "I'm paying you for a job. That's it. If I want a sermon, I'll wait for church on Sunday." Iris slammed down the phone.

She and Kurt had to hurry to get to the restaurant on time. When they finally arrived, they both looked worn out and nervous. Iris chain-smoked all the way there, and Kurt looked so zoned out that Iris momentarily wondered if he'd taken some of his special pain pills before he had hopped behind the steering wheel.

Jeff and Danni pulled up just as the Gradens were parking their car. Jeff was wearing a beautiful pair of Gucci pants and a crisp white shirt with a boldly colored tie. His dark blue jacket molded his broad shoulders to perfection. Danni gave him her most dazzling smile as he took her hand to help her from the car. She was wearing a dark blue dress and matching heels that suited her wonderfully.

Iris was stunned when she saw them. There was absolutely no denying what a gorgeous pair they made. He was so dark and handsome, and she was so fair and beautiful. They were almost of equal height, and it made them look even more spectacular together. But the thing that struck Iris the most was not how they looked together, but how they looked at each other. They were most definitely in love, and she was going to put a stop to that as soon as possible.

Danni finally took her attention from Jeff and noticed her approaching parents. Danni hugged her mother and introduced Jeff to her parents.

"Danni has told us about you," Iris said pointedly. Iris shook his hand limply.

Kurt extended his hand to Jeff. Although Jeff shook it respectfully and said all the right things, he momentarily fantasized about punching his lights out. Jeff knew he desperately needed God's help to restrain himself. He'd prayed about it that very afternoon.

Kurt attempted to make some small talk but looked like a jerk on the way into the restaurant.

Once seated, it was clear that Iris and Kurt were entirely out of their element. Jeff told them stories about growing up around the world. He told them about the various customs in Hawaii, Italy, France, and Greece. Danni was in stitches when he described trying to learn the different languages and customs and master the art of tying his shoes at the same time.

Iris and Kurt, however, were not amused. They had made up their minds ahead of time that they would not like Jeff, no matter how nice, polished, and handsome he was.

When their food arrived, both Jeff and Danni bowed their heads in prayer while Iris and Kurt just stared at them.

Once dessert was ordered, Danni excused herself to step to the restroom.

Kurt excused himself to step outside for "a breath of fresh air."

Jeff found himself alone at the table with Iris. "I'll get right to the point, Jeffy. I don't like you. I don't approve of you. I will do everything and anything to get you away from my daughter. She is *mine.*"

The hatred in the woman's eyes caused Jeff to almost scoot his chair back, just to put some distance between them. He realized she was utterly delusional. "I love her, Mrs. Graden. I don't understand why you hate me, but please, just give me a chance."

Iris curled her lip and used some colorful language that made Jeff blush.

Jeff refused to budge. "Danni has needed someone exactly like me in her life for a long time. I love her and I have been praying to meet someone like her. I'm sorry if you don't understand that."

"Yes, I can see you are one of those Jesus freaks. I'll bet Danni just loves that," Iris said sarcastically.

"I do love Jesus, Mrs. Graden, and I am glad that Danni and I have that in common," Jeff said as he regained his composure.

Just then, Danni returned to the table, and Kurt skulked back too. The stench of cigarette smoke attested to what he'd been up to.

Danni asked, "Did you two have lots to talk about while I was gone?"

"Loads," Iris said. Her voice bordered on sarcasm but didn't quite step over the line this time. She seemed to know just when she could push things and when to stop. She loved pushing things as far as they could go but had long since learned when to stop before she got herself into trouble. Usually. Now she was really going to have to use this technique to her advantage.

Mercifully, the dinner was soon over. Jeff said a formal and polite farewell to the Gradens. Never before had he been so thankful as he was that night to get away from someone. Not even the time in Rome when the chunky Italian opera diva had chased him down a side street, begging him for a little kiss.

11

"Well, what did you think of my parents? What did you and my mom talk about when I was in the powder room?" Danni asked once they were alone in the car.

Jeff leaned over and gently touched her cheek with his hand. She looked so sweet that he couldn't tell her exactly what he thought, at least not yet. Instead, he needed time to pray about it and just mentally absorb everything. "Well, they were certainly interesting," he said with a confidence he didn't really feel.

"I thought Mom was acting especially odd tonight, and Dad always does. I guess he really is rubbing off on her," Danni said. She exhaled and sighed deeply.

She went on to chat about their upcoming trip for Thanksgiving, and it made Jeff thankful he didn't tell her what he really thought of her parents. He silently prayed that Mrs. Graden would wise up before she did something stupid and hurt Danni even more than she already had.

Jeff and Danni spent as much time together as possible. Between their respective classes, her job at the bookstore, and his as editor of the *University Happenings*, it was tough to find time together, but they cherished every moment they had. Jana, LaMika, Sharon, and Dan were pleased to see the ongoing positive changes in Danni. They noticed her smiling more and bouncing around like a kangaroo. Her spirit seemed lighter than air.

Jeff was his usual happy self, only more so. He seemed more complete somehow. His friends—besides LaMika—Matt, Steve, and Derrick, rarely saw him anymore. They all liked Danni so much that it was hard to be upset with Jeff. They understood and supported him. Their friends soon couldn't remember a time when Jeff and Danni weren't together. It just felt right.

When the time to fly to Chicago arrived, Jeff was excited. Danni, on the other hand, couldn't have been less thrilled. Her nervous stomach got the best of her. She took two doses of Pepto Bismol. She was still so nervous about flying she just didn't think she could do it. Plus, Jeff was already too important to her, and she was frightened that his parents would hate her.

"I think I'll go to the bathroom one more time," Danni said, nearly in tears. She was positively green.

Jeff looked at her worriedly. He had arrived in high spirits, ready to drive them to the airport when he found Danni in a terrible state.

When she returned a few minutes later, she said sadly, "Maybe I should stay in Charlotte. I would hate to leave the apartment empty and all alone."

"Do you trust me?" Jeff asked her gently as she sat beside him. He looked into her eyes so tenderly that she couldn't force herself to look away.

"With my life," Danni said.

Jeff held out his hand, "Then, trust me now."

She gave his hand a squeeze, and they gathered her luggage and made their way downstairs and to his car. Before they pulled out of the parking lot, Jeff put his arm around Danni and prayed. "Dear Lord, You know Danni is not too excited about flying, and she's probably nervous about meeting my family. Please bless her and comfort her and help her have Your peace about it. Please help her to know that You have a great plan for her and won't let her down. Please help her to know that I love her too, and I won't hurt her. In the name of Jesus, Amen."

Danni wiped away tears and grinned at him. "Thank you," she said as they pulled away.

"That's what I'm here for," he said. "I'm at your service."

Once they were checked in and finally on the plane, Jeff said, "I'll be right beside you the whole time. Just squeeze my hand as hard as you need to." He silently hoped he wouldn't regret the offer, but he would have done just about anything to make Danni feel better. He didn't like seeing her so upset. As far as he was concerned, she'd been through enough of that.

The early-morning flight didn't have a lot of passengers, so they had the row to themselves, except for an elfin senior citizen, who was already snoring before the plane began to taxi down the runway.

As they began to roll down the runway, Jeff leaned over and said, "Hey, pretty lady, how about giving me a kiss?"

Danni's eyes grew big since she wasn't expecting it. When she recalled the moment later, she never knew for sure if the butterflies in her stomach were from the plane leaving the ground or her first real kiss. She literally saw stars as Jeff's lips gently met hers.

Jeff finally pulled back and looked at Danni, "If we keep that up, we will have to become frequent fliers."

Danni blushed furiously and, for once, didn't know what to say. Instead, she leaned her head on his shoulder and sighed, truly content and feeling ever so much better. "Thank You, Lord," she whispered, and Jeff smiled when he heard it.

The rest of the flight was uneventful and pleasant. Danni realized she shouldn't have been surprised because Jeff had a special way of making everything better.

Once they landed and disembarked, Jeff's parents, Connor and Rachel Kingston, nearly ran over the other loved ones waiting for their people to arrive. They couldn't wait to see their beloved son and meet the young lady who had captured his heart.

"Hi, Jeffy!" Rachel squealed and threw her arms around Jeff. Connor joined her a moment later. Very shortly, Rachel turned her attention to Danni.

"Mom, I'd like you to meet Danielle Graden," Jeff beamed.

Rachel extended her hand and exclaimed, "Danielle, I am so pleased to meet you. The way Jeff has talked about you, you'd think the two of you had known each other for ten years." She smiled warmly and it just lit up her whole face.

Rachel Kingston was a beautiful woman. She was also one of the few females who could almost look Danni in the eye. She had a soft, delicate face, framed by dark, shoulder-length hair cut in a trendy, chic style, a long, graceful neck, which was bathed in diamonds, and graceful arms and legs that seemed to stretch on endlessly as her full-length chocolate mink coat positively danced around her. Rachel's blue eyes were the image of Jeff's as she smiled and instantly made Danni feel welcome.

"Please, Mrs. Kingston, call me Danni."

"Only if you call me Rachel. I feel old enough, having a son as tall and handsome as Jeff. I don't want to feel one day older than is absolutely necessary!"

Danni laughed as Connor shook her hand. "Danni, I'm so glad to meet you. And, let's skip the formalities. Call me Connor." Connor Kingston was Jeff's height—a couple of inches over six feet. He had a lean, muscular build and looked very graceful. He even had the same stunning blue eyes as Jeff and Rachel. Together, the three of them made a striking trio. Danni felt energized just being with them. Like Jeff, Rachel and Connor made a point of including Danni in the conversation and made her glad she had been brave enough to come.

For just a moment, Danni felt a sharp pang of grief, missing Beth. Something about the lively and loving banter among the

Kingstons reminded Danni of Beth and her sweet family. But she silently asked God to help her put it out of her mind, so she could make room for making some happy memories.

After retrieving Jeff and Danni's things, they made their way to the sleek black limousine waiting outside. Connor and Rachel were busy getting everything settled and didn't see the look on Danni's face.

Jeff had totally forgotten his parents had rented a limo for the occasion. He squeezed her hand. "Remember, I'm right here. Everything will be okay. I love you."

Danni smiled appreciatively at him as they all slid into the limo. Rachel and Connor kept the conversation light and lively as they made their way to their house on the hill. She felt so at home with the Kingstons and blushed when she noticed Jeff watching her as she interacted with his parents. It was a wonderful, new feeling, and she relished every single moment of it.

The little house on a hill turned out to be a three-story estate, with twenty-three acres and two tennis courts, an indoor, Olympic-sized pool, eight bedrooms, six full bathrooms, and a whole host of other impressive amenities. Danni's jaw almost dropped when she saw it as the guard opened the heavy black gates. The limousine driver expertly maneuvered the car to the front door.

An elderly butler with a surprisingly jaunty step appeared to help them with the bags.

Jeff helped Danni from the car and hugged the butler. The two were clearly happy to see each other. "George, I would like to introduce you to Danni Graden. Danni, this is my favorite friend in the whole world, George."

George extended a wrinkled hand and smiled a very proper British smile. "I'm pleased to meet you," he said.

Jeff said, "George has been with my family since I was potty-trained. I'll bet he could be bribed into telling you a few good stories about me," he whispered as they made their way inside.

Connor and Rachel, who'd given Jeff and Danni a few moments to speak to George, moved in. Rachel said, "Jeff, I do hope you haven't been telling Danni all about what terrible bores we are," she said with such an exaggeratedly comical face that they all burst into spontaneous laughter, which felt really good to Danni.

"No, ma'am, I most certainly was not. I was, however telling her some stories about how wild and crazy George is," he replied with a completely straight face.

The subject of Jeff's outrageous statement had already gone ahead with their bags.

Connor and Rachel chuckled at the very idea of their proper English butler even thinking of doing anything remotely crazy.

Once in the foyer, Connor asked, "Danni, before you get settled in, would you like a tour?"

"Connor, I would be delighted," Danni replied. Danni was amazed by how open and warm and loving Jeff's parents were. However, it made her momentarily sad when she thought about the chilly reception her parents had given Jeff at their dinner together. They couldn't have been more different from the Kingstons.

As the foursome walked through the charming home, Danni was stunned. There were antiques and treasures from all over the world, spoils from extensive travel and living abroad. Each room had its own distinct theme.

The formal living room was dedicated to Australia. Old, leather-bound books lined a stone-encased bookshelf, and leather-bound rugs and furniture in beige and warm chocolates, almost matching Rachel's mink, were abundant in the room. A boomerang and Australian masks adorned the walls.

Across the magnificent hall, the formal dining room featured a Chinese theme. It had mirrors and fans and an ornate red and black silk screen. Danni saw that the beautiful table could seat twenty-four comfortably.

Next, they visited the kitchen to introduce Danni to the staff. She met three maids and the chef. The Kingstons clearly loved and appreciated their staff, and the feeling was certainly mutual, which warmed Danni's heart.

She had always wondered if rich people were all snobs, but clearly that wasn't the case here. Jeff was one of the most understated people she'd ever met. He appreciated the material blessings in his life, as did his family, but knew that wasn't what life was all about.

The kitchen was a hub of activity. Danni realized that the Kingstons' kitchen alone was about half the size of her parents' entire house. The kitchen had an enormous island in the middle, with various multi-colored pots and pans hanging from a pot rack. The floor was tiled in a friendly black-and-white pattern, which felt vaguely familiar, but Danni didn't know why.

Even from here, a stunning view of the grounds was evident throughout the large windows over the sink and prep area. The room reminded Danni of being in one of the far-away marketplaces she'd read about as the delicious aromas wafted her way.

The tour continued to the sweeping staircase. It made Danni feel like she was in *Gone With the Wind* as they ascended to the next floor.

Rachel, Jeff, and Connor helped Danni get settled into the room that would be hers for the visit. Danni's room happened to be next door to Jeff's old bedroom. Her room was full of cheery pale pink and green. A huge bay window gave a full view of the spectacularly manicured lawn and formal gardens, which appeared to stretch on endlessly.

After she got settled in, Danni took a tour of the gardens

with Rachel, while Connor visited with Jeff. As they strolled, Rachel smiled at Danni. "I think this is the happiest we've ever seen Jeff. We are so proud of him. You know, parents only want the best for their children. Jeff said you are an only child too, so I am sure you know what I mean."

Danni visibly winced, involuntarily inhaling sharply, but immediately tried to cover it up. An all-too-familiar stab of pain pricked her heart as she realized what she had wanted for so very long but had never had. She could only hope that Jeff would always appreciate what he had.

Rachel stopped and looked at her. "Oh, Danni, I am so sorry. I fear that I have just blazed on into a place where angels fear to tread."

"Oh, no. It's okay. I'm just not...close to my family," Danni said. "I never have been, but it is something that I always wanted." Danni attempted to put on a brave face so Rachel wouldn't see just how much she was hurting.

Rachel put an arm around Danni as they continued walking. "Well, perhaps I am becoming philosophical in my old age, but if they can't see how wonderful you are, then it's truly their loss. We are glad to have you with us. We have prayed for a long time for Jeff to meet someone special, and I am so glad it was you."

"Thank you, Rachel. I'm glad too." Danni returned Rachel's smile as they looked at the small lake filled with swans.

Thanksgiving lunch was an intimate but jovial affair. Jokes, stories, anecdotes, and the like filled the air. Again, the Kingstons made sure to include Danni, and she enjoyed herself immensely.

That evening, the Kingstons opened their home to host one hundred and fifty of their closest friends to "celebrate Thanksgiving properly," according to Connor. They had a full orchestra and a fountain flowing with champagne. It soon became a full-blown party, the likes of which Danni had never known. She was glad Jeff had warned her about it.

Jeff remained by her side the entire time, worried that she would be intimidated. She was, in fact, but no one except Jeff ever knew it. They laughed and talked and danced all night long. Jeff proudly introduced her to everyone.

As they danced, he held her close and didn't ever want to let her go. Although she loved the holiday, she still worried about Iris. Connor and Rachel had generously told her to call her family and talk as long as she wanted to, which she appreciated.

Jeff escorted her to his father's study and stayed, at her request, while she called home. Her palms were damp as she dialed the number. "Hi, Mom. Happy Thanksgiving," she said cheerily when Iris answered.

"Well, I hope you're happy," Iris retorted. "Your father is so sad you are not here that he and Ruby couldn't even eat dinner with me. Instead, I ate it all alone, while you're up there having a grand old time." Her voice sounded pathetic and whiny.

"I'm sorry, Mom. I just wanted to wish you a 'Happy Thanksgiving' and see how you are. The Kingstons are having a few people over, so I need to go."

Jeff shot her a mischievous grin at that understatement.

"I'll call you on Sunday when the plane lands," Danni offered. This was the first time they were to go several days without talking on the phone. Danni, for one, was glad to have that break from Iris.

"Whatever," Iris mumbled and hung up.

Jeff hugged Danni once she finished talking with Iris. "I'm sure that was hard," he said sympathetically. "I don't understand the dynamics of your family, but I can tell it's not your fault," he said. "Everything will be okay."

Not wanting to tempt themselves by being alone too long, Jeff quickly suggested they return to the party, which was in full swing. He respected Danni too much to make a foolish mistake, although he admitted to himself that he just couldn't resist kissing her when he had the chance.

The rest of the visit with the Kingstons was a wonderful, magical time Danni knew she would never forget. As she hugged Connor and Rachel at the airport, tears threatened to ruin her makeup. She relished the simple act of hugging them because it made her feel normal and loved.

The flight back to Charlotte was smooth. Although Danni still wasn't keen on flying, this time was much easier than the first.

That night, Danni dreamed about Jeff taking her away to a beautiful castle. She dreamed of the most magnificent party. It was a delightful dream, one from which she didn't want to awaken.

Russell called Danni early the next day, which was a rare treat indeed. He had very limited access to phone service in Kenya, which is where he was stationed with the Water of Life Christian Outreach Mission. The work was hard, he said, but he loved it. After they chatted a bit, he said, "Danni, I've got some news, and I thought you'd want to hear it from me."

Danni's heart slammed in her chest in an uncomfortable rhythm. She knew the tone of Russell's voice, and it wasn't good. "Okay..."

"It's about Andy. He just felt overwhelmed as he's gone through the surgeries and therapy. He fell in with the wrong crowd and got into drugs. He got arrested last week and is in jail for holding up a liquor store while he and his thug buddies were high."

"Oh, no, not another friend," Danni sobbed. "I have to go out there. I've got to go help him." She hastily dashed away the river of tears now flowing down her face.

"Danni, you can't," Russell said. "They are only letting his parents and his attorney see him. It's a real mess," Russell said. Their connection was beginning to break up, and Danni felt so far removed from both him and Andy. They talked for only a brief moment more, then the connection was broken.

Thankfully, Jeff and Danni both had a free evening, so he took her out for hot chocolate so they could talk. Jeff was a great listener, and Danni really appreciated that about him.

12

Time flew by as they moved toward semester exams. Jeff and Danni were closer than ever. They were both excellent students, like Jana. Sharon stuck her tongue out at all of them and did her best to skate by so she could stay in school and be near her precious Dan.

Jeff and Danni brought out the best in each other, and they each encouraged the other to work hard. Danni had happily agreed to spend Christmas with the Kingstons. Iris had raged and cried and done everything she could to make Danni come home to Mountainview, but she refused. Instead, Danni bought Iris a pretty scarf and a pair of earrings, wrote a poem, and mailed everything in a care package. She got small gifts for Kurt and Ruby out of a sense of obligation but never received any acknowledgment. Danni was only hoping for a card, but one never came.

As Jeff and Danni reached the airport this time, she felt sadness mixed with relief. At least she wouldn't be lonely this Christmas like she had been every other Christmas before.

This time, Jana had insisted on driving them to the airport. "It's the only way I get to see the two of you," she laughed. Jeff and Danni had loaded Jana down with Christmas packages before leaving the apartment. Jana, Sharon, and Dan were touched by Jeff's generosity. He never bragged about it but seemed truly grateful and loved to share with others.

"Jana, I'm telling you, you and your family must come up to visit my family sometime. My parents live for entertaining. Besides, you need to meet some of my friends up there. You'd love them," Jeff said.

Jana's eyes widened. "If you'd told me that sooner, I'd have gone too. You're such a rat, Jeff. Shame on you!" Jana said, laughing.

Janna dropped them off, waved goodbye, and was gone. They checked in and didn't have to wait long before they were happily settled on the plane. "I think Jana is really worried about Sharon too," Jeff said.

Danni sighed. "She was so trying hard to be full of Christmas cheer that I didn't want to bring it up. I've been busy with you and work and Bible study and exams, so I haven't really seen Sharon as much as I normally would. But something is definitely wrong. Jana said she called Dan the other day, at his work, just to check on Sharon, to see if he knew what was wrong. He didn't seem to know either, but he sounded really sad," Danni said.

"Do you think she and Dan are having problems?" Jeff asked. "I haven't spent a lot of time alone with him, but the few times we went to play basketball at the gym, he seemed fine," Jeff said.

"I agree. I think whatever the problem is, Sharon may have kept it from Dan too."

"Whatever it is, we are going to enjoy our holiday, pray for them, and help if we can," Jeff said, squeezing her hand.

They fell into a pensive silence and finally began to talk of other things. The plane landed smoothly, much to Danni's relief. She couldn't imagine ever loving to fly, but she was trying to prayerfully embrace it.

Connor and Rachel were there to greet them, Connor himself having just returned from a business trip to Tokyo. Rachel was in a twitter over the arrival of everyone. Danni correctly guessed that she had been running around all day, making sure everything was perfect for their arrival, which made her smile.

And it was. A gloriously decorated tree was front and center in the massive foyer. It was nothing short of gorgeous, laden with ornaments the Kingstons had picked up from their extensive travels. Twinkling lights were so bright that Danni thought they could have been used to successfully land a small airplane. Rachel and Connor had certainly outdone themselves.

George the butler greeted them warmly and took their things. "Nice to see you again, Miss Danni," he said with a smile. He winked at Jeff.

Jeff and Danni followed his parents into the living room for tea and settled in for a nice visit. Connor told them a hilarious story about how he almost missed his flight when the lady with whom he was sharing a cab suddenly went into labor, and the driver had to detour to the hospital.

When everyone went upstairs to change for dinner, Danni closed the door to the guest room and felt like she needed to pinch herself. She thanked God for showing her that she actually was worthy of being loved and what being part of a family was really like. She sighed contentedly and prayed this feeling would last.

After dinner, Rachel hugged Danni and said, "Since I never had the blessing of having a daughter, I hope you'll indulge me."

Danni hugged her back and said, "I'd like nothing more." She didn't think she'd be able to say anything else; her heart was so happy. Danni blinked rapidly several times, just to make sure no unwanted tears crept out.

Christmas was a grand affair. It made the Kingstons' Thanksgiving celebration pale in comparison. Yet, they made a point of keeping Jesus front and center. On Christmas Day, they and all their guests sang "Happy Birthday" to Jesus, and they served a grand five-layer cake with "Happy Birthday, Jesus!" on it.

Danni had never seen that done before, and its significance

brought tears to her eyes. At that moment, Danni couldn't imagine being anywhere else in the whole world and didn't want to. Even the tears Danni had cried lately were almost all happy, which was a welcome new feeling for her.

13

Later in the day, more friends came over to celebrate. After their little get-together, Rachel and Connor said they were going to volunteer at the local soup kitchen, which Danni thought was terrific.

"Do you want to join us, or would you like a break?" Rachel asked. Danni had told them about her work at the mission in Charlotte.

"I'd love to go, "Danni said.

"I think that's a great idea," Jeff agreed as they all got their coats, hats, gloves, and scarves. It was bone-chilling cold, so they had to bundle up.

Danni thought about Jake, Carla, and Carla's sorry excuse for a boyfriend, Harvey. She prayed for each of them. Carla had really touched her heart. Danni thought it was at least partially because Carla reminded her of herself. If she hadn't received the scholarship, she didn't know where she would be now. Oh, how she longed to help Carla.

After they returned from the soup kitchen, Jeff suggested they call her family while Rachel and Connor went to check on things in the kitchen. Iris was her usual, unpleasant self.

"I lied and told everyone you had the flu when they asked where you were." Iris was practically snarling at her daughter. "I just can't believe you're parading around with that boy so flagrantly!"

"Mom, you don't have to lie," Danni said, fighting to remain calm. "The truth is kind, especially when it involves someone you love."

"Let me talk to that boy," Iris demanded, refusing to even use his name.

"Hi. Mrs. Graden. Merry Christmas," Jeff said.

"Merry Christmas, my foot," Iris said. "I'm going to kill you. I mean it. Leave my daughter alone, or you'll both be very sorry!" Iris sounded so pathetic that he had a hard time taking her seriously.

"Well, it was nice talking to you too," he said sweetly, refusing to take the bait, which raised Iris's blood pressure a few points.

Once they'd broken the connection, Jeff asked, "Are you glad that's over?"

"Yes, I shouldn't feel that way, I know, but..."

"Correction. You shouldn't have to feel that way. Now, cheer up, I haven't given you your main Christmas present yet. I don't know where my manners are," Jeff said, smiling proudly.

"Do you dare tease me!" Danni said. "You and your parents have already spoiled me."

"Nonsense," Jeff said. "Now, be a good girl and close your eyes."

Danni did as she was told as he led her by the hand.

"Open your eyes now," he said, once they had arrived at their destination.

Danni's mouth dropped open as she saw a brand-new white Mercedes with a huge purple bow on top.

"It's all yours. Merry Christmas," Jeff said excitedly.

"Oh, Jeff, I love it!" Danni said, jumping up and down and clapping her hands. She threw her arms around his neck and hugged him tightly. "Thank you! I love you," she said, planting a big kiss on his cheek.

He handed her the keys and said, "Let's go for a ride."

Once they were settled in, Danni said, "There's a mistake. It's a stick shift. I can't drive it."

"No, mistake. You've got to learn to drive it, so let's roll."

Danni growled but tried her best. It took seven tries, but she finally got it started. She stalled it in the circular driveway and almost took out the driveway's focal point, a large marble fountain in the shape of an angel.

"I think you made the angel tinkle," Jeff said.

"If I weren't so busy trying not to crash, I'd have to get you for that one, Kingston," Danni said.

Connor and Rachel were smiling and watching from an upstairs window. They loved Danni dearly and were so happy for the joy she brought to Jeff.

Although it was bitterly cold, there was currently no snow on the ground, which was very rare for that time of year. So, Jeff suggested they drive around the neighborhood.

"How will we get it back to Charlotte?" Danni asked.

"I took the liberty of not booking return tickets back to Charlotte. I figured we could just drive it back. Anytime you need a break or feel uncomfortable, I can take over," Jeff offered.

It was hard to leave Connor and Rachel when it was time to go. Danni was very attached to them. They had sent their Christmas gifts to Charlotte, realizing very little would fit into the car. Danni and Jeff giggled because they were both so tall they had to fold up a bit to fit, but it was Danni's dream car, and Jeff had been determined to bless her with it.

It was a long drive, so they set out early. Jeff handled all of the big city driving, as Danni put it, and any places where the weather made it tricky. When they finally got back to Danni's apartment, Danni was thrilled to find Jana happily visiting with Sharon and Dan, both of whom looked like they didn't have a care in the world.

Jana, Sharon, and Dan all rushed out to the parking lot to admire Danni's new car. Jana grumbled to Jeff that he'd really let her down by not bringing her a six-foot-two present back to Charlotte, which made everyone laugh.

"Jana, wait a minute," Danni said as the light went on in her head. "Is this why you didn't say anything about picking us up from the airport?" Danni asked.

"Well..." Jana shrugged her shoulders with a mischievous smile.

The next day was New Year's Eve, so Jeff, Danni, and all their friends went to dinner at La Maison. Dan and Sharon were both in high spirits, and Jana brought a cute guy from her philosophy class. LaMika and her beau of the week came, along with Jeff's buddies, Matt, Steve, Derrick, and their respective dates. They all had a relaxing time.

Afterward, they all drove up to the lake house and had a great party to ring in the next year. They enjoyed each other's company immensely, and when it was time to go home, they drove extra carefully to avoid the drunk people who seemed to not care if they were driving under the influence.

Jeff took Danni out the next day and stunned her when he said, "If I can get a halfway decent job with Altemonte Publishing, I'm going to prove that I can make it own my own without my parents' help."

He held up a finger when Danni started to say something. "My parents are great, but their material success is theirs. I love them and appreciate their help, but I'm going to be successful in my own right. As soon as I do that, I want you to be my wife."

He got down on one knee and presented her with a stunning sapphire promise ring. "This is my promise to you," he said and slipped it on her finger. "I know it's fast, but when it's right, it's right. You are the answer to my prayers."

Danni's eyes were wide with delight. She smiled and nodded and hugged him tightly. And with that, it was settled. They both looked forward to the future with a joy that neither of them had thought possible.

The semester flew by. Jana had a string of cute boyfriends, but there was always something wrong with each one. One loved to wear sandals but had a crooked toe that was a deal-breaker for her; one had ears that were too pointy, which reminded her of an elf; and one had shoulders that were simply too square for her taste. Sharon got edgy once again, and this time, so did Dan. Amid it all, Danni and Jeff were happier than ever. The promise ring never left her finger.

As the school year drew to a close, Jana moved back in with her parents for the summer, as did Sharon. Danni, who wanted to be near Jeff and as far from Mountainview as possible, opted to go to summer school, as did Jeff. They both wanted to graduate early so they could get married. The apartment was quiet without Sharon and Jana that summer.

Jeff and Danni both took several classes, worked, continued with Bible study, and Danni continued volunteering at the mission. Jeff joined her whenever possible, and he really enjoyed helping the people. He had such an easygoing manner that people just naturally opened up to him. She admired that about him and tried to be more like that, but it didn't come naturally for her. After the sheer terror she'd lived with for so many years, being easygoing didn't come easily to her at all. But Jeff was doing a superb job of helping her find the fun in life, so she had hope of things changing.

Rachel and Connor flew down in June for a visit. They stayed at the lake house, and Danni spent as much time with them as possible. They both rolled up their sleeves and volunteered at the mission twice during their visit.

Rachel, like Danni, adored sweet Carla. Rachel had an overwhelming mom instinct that made her just want to reach out and hug people. She was so genuine that it naturally drew people to her. Carla loved her and wanted to hang around with Rachel and Danni.

"Is that your boyfriend?" Carla asked as she sat with Rachel and Danni, observing Connor and Jeff on the other side of the room. The guys were busy setting up for a fresh wave of hungry people.

"Yes," Danni said with a smile, "And this is his wonderful mom, Rachel."

"I can tell he loves you," Carla said with a sad smile. "He can't take his eyes off of you."

"I love him too," Danni said. Although her heart wanted to burst with joy, she was sensitive to Carla, who was clearly in a world of hurt.

"I wish somebody would look at me like that," she said sadly. "Harvey never will."

"You can leave him," Rachel said, gently putting her hand over Carla's and giving it a squeeze.

"No, I can't," Carla said, letting the tears fall.

"We can get you some help," Danni offered, not wanting to push her but desperate to help.

"I've gotta go," Carla said, hurriedly grabbing her meager belongings. "Thank you for the food and for talking to me," she said, wiping her tears. She gathered the little bag of extra food Danni had packed for Harvey and hurried out the door. Even though it was summer, Carla looked like she was wearing all of the clothes she owned. A number of people who came through the mission did that. It was bulky for sure, but the people were terrified that what few belongings they had in their possession would get stolen. It was a rotten way to live.

A part of Danni's heart broke for Carla as she watched her go. "Danni, I'm really proud of you," Rachel said.

"Thank you. That could have been me so easily," Danni said, fighting back the tears. She had long-since confided her situation to Rachel, who had sobbed over it. Danni dabbed at her eyes and shook her head.

"No, Danni. It could never have been you. You have more fight in you than just about anyone I have ever known. You keep fighting. You keep going no matter what," Rachel said as she put her arm around Danni's shoulders.

14

Iris found a pitiful excuse to call Danni nearly every night. She still hadn't forgiven Danni for not coming home for the summer, but she seemed somewhat appeased to call her every day. No matter what time of day, Danni could look at the clock and know exactly what was happening back at the Graden home. Danni vowed to never let her life turn out that way.

Everything was so routine, so sad. It physically hurt Danni to know that the mom whose love was always just out of her reach had finally settled into a place where Danni realized that Iris had all but given up.

Jeff saw Danni's pain. It hurt him deeply, and as much as he wanted to fix it, he knew he couldn't. So, he kept praying for her, encouraging her, and loving her.

Jeff took Danni on picnics and sailing, and he loved to take her shopping. She always felt guilty about the shopping and only let him do it for her once in a while. She wanted to be clear that she loved him for who he was, not what he had.

One evening, Danni and Jeff were finishing dinner and getting set to play cards at her apartment when Jana called, frantic and crying. Danni was busy washing dishes, so she asked Jeff to answer the phone. Jana told them to put on the evening news, said a few things to Jeff, and promptly hung up.

Jeff turned on the news, and they sat watching a horrible drama unfold before them. A famous reporter shoved a microphone in Sharon's mother's face as Sharon and Dan tried to shield her from the cameras and the never-ending questions of the press.

The reporter's unemotional voice said, "Millionaire tycoon, Patrick J. Bane, was arrested today, as stunned family members watched. Bane is charged with statutory rape and embezzlement of thirty million dollars from the Children's Well-Being Organization. No bond has been allowed at this time. If convicted, Bane could face fifty years in prison with no chance of parole..." the reporter's voice droned on.

To Danni and Jeff, the lives of what appeared to be such a sweet family had just been torn apart forever. Danni began to cry as Jeff held her. "How could they say such terrible things?" Danni asked.

Jeff shook his head and didn't know what to say. He, like Danni, was just too stunned. Jeff had met Sharon's parents several times, and he really liked them. Pat and Darla Bane were involved in Sharon's life and wanted to know her friends. They seemed to truly love their family, so this was all unbelievable

"I don't know what to say except that we can go down first thing tomorrow if you want. Jana is going down and she thought you'd want to go too," Jeff explained.

Although Pat and Darla lived primarily in Hilton Head, Pat's business was headquartered in Charlotte, so they came often and checked in with Sharon while they were there. Pat was currently sitting in jail in downtown Charlotte, which seemed unthinkable.

"Yes, let's do that. I can't believe it. This certainly explains Sharon's odd behavior as of late," Danni marveled.

Jeff suggested, "I have an idea. I can call my parents and talk to them about the situation. They have a great team of attorneys. I'll see if they can give us some advice."

"Thank you, Jeff. You're the best," Danni said. She sniffed and dried her tears. She couldn't help but smile when he kissed the top of her head and handed her a tissue.

Jeff called Connor, and he agreed to see what could be done to help. He had heard about it already and thought it was a heart-breaking situation.

Bright and early the next morning, Jana arrived in her parents' old station wagon, which was now running well, thanks to a recent trip to the auto body repair shop. Jeff and Danni hopped into Jana's roomy ride as she filled them in on what she knew of the situation.

"The police have had Mr. Bane under surveillance for months. Sharon, Dan, and Darla must be terribly upset. They must have had at least some kind of clue that something was wrong. Now we know why Sharon has been so upset," Jana said as she maneuvered through traffic.

"Did Sharon ever mention anything about this?" Jeff asked, his brow furrowed.

"No," Danni replied as Jana shook her head. "I can't get my head around it. I wonder who Sharon and Dan talked to. I know it certainly wasn't us."

Danni felt sad that Sharon hadn't confided in her, then immediately felt guilty because she had been so wrapped up in her own life that she hadn't been there for Sharon. But now wasn't the time for that. Now was the time to make sure she concentrated on helping Sharon and her family through this nightmare.

Jana pulled up to the entrance to the Banes' Lake Wylie home. It was surrounded by stunning trees and a sprawling lawn. The house itself was built from stone, and the front facade was crawling with ivy. Danni knew Sharon's family was from a high station in life, but she never realized just how high until now. She only hoped that it didn't mean Sharon's father had farther to fall.

The maid warily answered the door when they rang the bell.

Sharon burst into tears when she saw her friends. She hugged them hard, as did Dan, who was equally thankful to see some friendly faces.

Dan said, "Robert Anderson just left. He had a business emergency and had to leave. I'm sorry you missed him. I want all of our real friends to get to know each other." As he said it, Dan glanced over to Danni. For some reason, she felt a chill. It was totally ridiculous, she chastised herself, immediately feeling guilty. This Robert Anderson was supposed to be a knight in shining armor. Besides, she had Jeff, and that was all she cared about. He was her knight in shining armor.

Darla Bane was glad Sharon and Dan's friends had come too. Everything was moving at lightning speed. The trial was already promising to be lengthy and ugly. Darla's eyes, like Sharon's, were red and puffy. No one looked like they'd had any sleep in some time.

Danni and Jana took Sharon for a walk around the property while Dan talked to Jeff, and Darla went to return some phone calls. Sharon didn't say much. The girls tried to cheer her up but to no avail.

"I talked to Daddy," Sharon said sadly. "He kept saying he was so sorry that it all came out like it did. He admitted it was all true. I can't believe it."

Sharon made it to a nearby stone bench, sat down, and sobbed like a small child who had lost her favorite toy. But, in fact, she had lost so much more. Pat Bane had been her hero. They held him up on such a high pedestal that the fall he had just taken had broken his entire family.

Jana and Danni sat down on either side of Sharon and looked at each other for a moment over Sharon's head, not quite sure what to do or say.

Meanwhile, Jeff talked quietly with Dan in the Banes' study.

"Pat admitted to us that it's true. I thought Sharon would die at the news. She has always been especially close to Pat, and I don't think she had a clue. Actually, none of us did," Dan said sadly. He blew out a breath and shook his head.

Jeff patted Dan on the shoulder. "I know this is difficult, to say the least, but I am thankful Sharon and Darla have you." Jeff had never been in such a situation. He really wanted to help, but this was something he felt totally unprepared for. "Do you want me to pray with you?" he asked.

With tears in his eyes, Dan said, "Yes. I think I need that. I think we all do."

So, Jeff and Dan prayed together and asked for God's healing, guidance, and mercy all over this situation and for all of the people involved.

Later that day, Jeff slipped to the phone and called Connor. The news was not good. His team of lawyers said there was little they could do. After reviewing the information, they realized that Patrick Bane had been given just enough of the proverbial rope to hang himself, and he had done an excellent job of it. He had been sloppy and careless and barely bothered covering up the evidence of his misdeeds. He had left an easily visible trail for the authorities to follow.

15

The visible trail turned out to be Pat's downfall. Motel receipts under his own name, photographs, and various other painful reminders of Pat's stupidity were plastered all over the news for days. It was a media circus. Mercifully, the trial was swift in coming and didn't last long.

Pat was found guilty on all counts and sentenced to fifty years plus full restitution to all the people who had lost their life savings, thanks to Pat. In what seemed like a matter of hours, he was suddenly shipped out of state to a prison where he would spend his last days on earth.

Darla adjusted better than Sharon. Darla came from an impoverished family in rural South Carolina and had been working full-time for several years by the time she met Pat. Those lean early years helped her appreciate all of the material comforts she enjoyed with him.

Darla made some phone calls, and within a short time, she had a job, something she hadn't had to think of in years. Dan helped her find a small apartment in a neighboring town. The others helped her move, and Sharon decided to join her, at least for a while, until things settled down. She took a break from school, which everyone knew meant she probably would not be returning.

With sad hearts, after the last box had been moved into the new apartment, Jana, Danni, and Jeff said goodbye to Darla and Sharon. Gone were the merry wars of apartment 307. In a short time, Sharon had lost the rock of their family, the man who had been her lifelong hero. It turned out that nobody had known him at all. Sharon's brother was so stunned and grief-stricken that he couldn't fly home from Paris yet. He was a mess. He was hoping to get home soon to be with Darla and Sharon.

Dan found a job and an apartment closer to Darla and Sharon. His parents, who'd never liked Sharon, had given him an ultimatum—either break up with her, or he could kiss them goodbye forever. He had already made a commitment to Sharon in his heart, so he walked away without looking back. It was so cruel and unfair of Dan's parents to try to do that to him, especially during such a painful time for Sharon and her family. It really highlighted how heartless they were.

Soon, life settled back down, and they all found a new groove. The rest of the summer passed quickly and uneventfully. Danni, Jeff, and Jana were glad when the new semester started. They just weren't prepared for any more surprises.

Danni squealed with delight when she ran into LaMika on the first day of the fall semester that year. LaMika never failed to bring a smile to Danni's face. Danni grabbed LaMika and gave her a great big bear hug.

"Grandmama spent the whole time trying to get me to learn her ways, mon. It is just no good, I'm tellin ya. It's no good. Between you and Jeff, I'm wanting to hear more about Jesus. I think He is the way to go," LaMika said.

"Oh, that is music to my ears!" Danni exclaimed. "And He *is* the way to go." Danni gave LaMika the information about when and where to meet for the Bible study she and Jeff both loved.

Before they knew it, their time at university was rapidly coming to a close. LaMika had committed herself to Jesus and was at peace. She was in the process of completing her nursing degree under the staff at University Hospital. Jana had completed her remaining coursework and found a teaching position with a nearby school system, teaching and coaching the girls' basketball team.

The youngest of the bunch, Danni was beginning her student teaching assignment at a local high school and planning to get her degree at the end of the semester. Jeff had been offered a fabulous position with the Kane-Ridge Agency, one of the most prestigious advertising agencies in the country. It was the answer to a lot of prayer.

Jeff hadn't told anyone yet. The first thing he did was go and pick out an exquisite three-carat engagement ring for Danni. He'd had his eye on it for a long, long time. Under different circumstances, Jeff would have asked Kurt and Iris for their blessing. But that was not to be in this case. Iris had harassed Danni the whole time Jeff had known her. It was never going to change, and Danni had done her best to accept it. Kurt was downright weird, and Ruby was no better.

Jeff had gone to Mountainview with Danni once during her sophomore year for a brief visit. It had been such an absolute disaster that they had not returned since. Danni only saw Iris occasionally when Iris was willing to drive to Charlotte. Iris still tried to call and bother Danni every day, and Danni said that was better than having to see her in person.

By now, Danni had become a beloved fixture with the Kingstons, and they loved having her visit as often as possible. They were the family she'd always wanted, and the love was clearly mutual.

Jeff met Danni at her new apartment at the end of her fourth week of student teaching. Now that Jana had graduated, Danni was all alone for her final semester and had moved to a one-bedroom apartment just off campus. Sharon had decided not to return to college. Instead, she had found a job and insisted on staying with her mom for a while to help her. Dan stayed close by, and even though they'd had to put their marriage plans on hold, Dan was optimistic that everything would turn out well.

"Whew! What a week! Only six more to go," Danni said with relief. She popped off her shoes and wrinkled her nose as she accidentally took a whiff of her feet. Danni had been offered a job at the high school where she was completing her student teaching only the week before. She was starting in January, and she was excited and nervous.

Jeff rolled his eyes and grinned. He adored her, but he had learned not to get too close to her shoes after she'd been wearing them for a while. He was so excited about his secret that he didn't think he could keep it much longer. "Danni, get changed into something casual. I've got a surprise for you," he said, refusing to give anything away, even when she pestered him.

Danni hurried to change into jeans and a pretty red sweater Rachel had given her. It was one of Danni's favorites. She brushed her hair until it gleamed and quickly braided it. Some tendrils escaped and framed her face beautifully. Danni's skin had cleared up so much that no one would have known acne had ever plagued her. Unfortunately, though, when she got nervous, she still struggled with stomach issues. She dabbed on a bit of lip gloss and was ready to go.

"Okay, where are we going, sir?" Danni asked playfully as she sailed back into the living room.

"Not going to tell," Jeff said. "Let's go, young lady," he said, ushering her out the door.

Jeff drove to the opposite side of town and turned down a road that led to an airfield.

"Okay, what in the world are we doing?" Danni asked.

"Hang on a minute," Jeff said slyly. "Good things come to those who wait."

Jeff parked and helped Danni from the car. He led her around the back of the hangar where she was surprised to see a huge hot air balloon. It had red, white, blue, purple, green, and pink vertical stripes. The hot air balloon attendant was prepping it for take-off. "There's our ride," he said.

Danni was impressed. She still didn't love flying of any kind, although she'd had enough practice visiting the Kingstons in Chicago for the last few years. However, she was definitely growing much more comfortable with it.

"This is a nice surprise," Danni stammered.

"Well, I'm glad you like it," Jeff said. "Come on, let's get in."

A few minutes later, they were lifting off. Jeff pulled her close and said, "Danni, I love you. You are the answer to a lot of prayer. I couldn't have dreamed up a more ideal woman than you. Will you please make me the happiest man in the world and marry me?" With that, he carefully got down on one knee and produced the box containing the engagement ring.

Danni's eyes immediately filled with tears. Her mouth dropped open, and she squealed, "Yes! Yes! Yes!" She was so excited she was shaking when he slid the ring on her finger. She hugged him and wanted to jump up and down but then remembered they were up in a hot air balloon, so jumping up and down probably wasn't the best plan.

Instead, she kissed him, something they didn't do a lot. They wanted to but had managed to keep the relationship on a level that honored God. They'd each found accountability partners and answered to them on a regular basis. Jeff promised himself they would do things the right way. And, even though it wasn't always easy, they both had agreed it would be worth it.

Jeff smiled at Danni. "I was thinking that if you wanted to, we could get married just before Christmas, have our honeymoon, and you could be ready to start teaching in January. That way it wouldn't interfere with your school schedule." He then told her about his job with the Kane-Ridge Agency.

Danni said, "That is absolutely perfect. A Christmas wedding. Wait, that's not too long from now. Oh, my. There are so many things to do and plan. How will we get it all done?"

Jeff laughed at Danni's enthusiasm. "Would you relax? You have said, 'Yes,' now the hard part is over. Everything else will be easy."

"Did you really think I would turn you down?" Danni asked as she arched an eyebrow.

As the balloon gently descended, Jeff put an arm around her. "I was hoping you'd agree, but proposing marriage is scary. I'm glad you only have to do it once."

"Me too," Danni agreed.

Jeff had reserved a table at La Maison. They had a wonderful dinner and talked about the wedding. They then drove back to Danni's apartment and began calling everyone to share the wonderful news.

First, they called Connor and Rachel. "Yes!" Rachel shouted. "I knew it! I just knew it!"

Connor also sent his congratulations before Rachel snatched the phone back from him. She was beside herself with joy. "When is the wedding? Can we give you an engagement party? How can we help?" The happy questions went on and on.

The Kingstons knew that Danni would never be close to her family, and over the years, they had stepped in and truly became family to her. Now it was going to become official! They could barely contain their excitement. They had always been sad that no more children had arrived after Jeff, so Danni had become the daughter they had always wanted.

After Jeff and Danni hung up the phone, Rachel and Connor uncorked a bottle of champagne and danced the night away. They were beside themselves with joy. They were happy when Jeff told them about his new job, but that took a backseat to the wedding news, and Jeff thought that was just the way it should be.

Jeff and Danni selected December 17 as their wedding date. Danni would finish her student teaching the week before. They would have plenty of time to honeymoon and get settled into married life before she had to begin teaching in January.

When Jeff had accepted his job offer, he made sure his new employer would agree to his plan. Jeff was brilliant, so Mr. Kane-Ridge had no qualms about helping him with his plans. Besides, Mr. Kane-Ridge was quite the romantic himself, so he simply couldn't turn down a young man in love.

Jeff had even pointed out to Danni that with his income, they could pay off her scholarship, and she wouldn't have to teach, if she didn't want to. It would free her up to write, which was her true passion. She'd always loved writing, but Iris had degraded her at every opportunity for so long, that Danni's confidence was severely wounded.

Danni told Jeff she would need to pray about it. She didn't want him to feel like she was mooching off him. Jeff always loved doing things for Danni; he just wished she would let him do more.

"Jeff, I hope you know that I am so proud of you. I knew you could do it," Danni said about Jeff's new job. She was happy for him, for both of them. Danni understood how much Jeff wanted to make it on his own. He didn't want to be dependent on his parents, unable to exist without them, as Sharon had been. The very idea frightened him. Now, he had landed the job on his own, and he thanked God for it.

Jana and LaMika were thrilled when Jeff and Danni shared their news. They also happily accepted when Danni asked them to be her bridesmaids. She wanted to ask Sharon to be part of the wedding party too, but when Danni called her, she sounded so sad. They knew she couldn't afford it, and there was no way she would let Danni and Jeff help.

Jeff had asked Connor to be his best man, and Steve, Matt, and Derrick all happily agreed to be his groomsmen.

Finally, the only phone call left to make was to the Gradens. Neither wanted to do it, but it was necessary. "Hi, Mom," Danni said tentatively when Iris answered the phone.

"Well, I thought my only daughter was dead," Iris said. "I haven't been able to talk to you in two whole days. I can't believe it. You just ran off to school with that boy, and—"

Danni cut her off. She was simply not going to let Iris ruin her happy moment. This was too special. "Mom, Jeff proposed to me. I accepted, and we are getting married on December seventeenth."

"Oh, I see," Iris said. She didn't know what else to say. She was at a loss for words for once. Their conversation was short and clipped, and thankfully it was soon over. Iris hurriedly hung up without a word of love or kindness or congratulations for Danni and Jeff. She had much more important things on her mind.

A few days later, Jeff and Danni drove over to Jana's apartment. She'd said she had some wedding ideas she wanted to share with them and had asked them to stop by. It was still weird for Danni that she and Jana were no longer roommates, but since

Jana had graduated, she'd moved out. Thankfully, she wasn't too far away, and Jeff and Danni had already picked out a cute townhouse near downtown. Everything was falling into place quickly!

When they rang the doorbell, it sounded like a flurry of activity inside, but Jeff and Danni didn't think much of it. A moment later, the door flew open and a chorus of voices rang out, "Surprise! Surprise!" Jana and LaMika had organized a surprise party for the happy couple. There were hugs and kisses all around.

The tiny apartment was decorated in white, purple, and green—the couple's chosen wedding colors. It was a great party, and everyone had a wonderful time. Danni still couldn't believe that Jeff Kingston was going to be her husband. She loved him with every fiber of her being. He always said she was the answer to his prayers, and he was most certainly the answer to hers.

The entire next week was something out of a dream. Everyone congratulated Jeff and Danni. Connor and Rachel called four times, asking what they could do next to help. In a matter of days, Danni had selected her wedding dress, the bridesmaids' dresses, the cake, flowers, booked the church, and attended to many other details.

Even her students were thrilled for her when she showed them her heart-shaped engagement ring. She was more than a little tired, but she couldn't ever remember being as happy in her life. She knew she never would be again. Nothing could top this. Danni felt on top of the world as she hopped in her Mercedes to go to school.

On a Friday afternoon in November, not long before Thanksgiving, Jana came over to Danni's apartment to go over some final wedding details. Jeff had to work late on a new advertising campaign, so he was going to take some work to the lake house so he could really concentrate on it and planned to take Danni and Jana out for a late dinner at one of their favorite hangouts in town.

"Goodness gracious, are you getting married, or are you planning an invasion by the fashion police?" Jana asked, in mock horror, as Danni came back from her bedroom, trying to balance an armload of fabric samples, pictures, and pamphlets in her arms. Before her friend could help, Danni dropped them in a graceless heap onto the dining room table. They both laughed at the mess she had so easily created.

"I think I'm doing a bit of both," Danni said with a grin.

"Has your mom said anything else about the wedding?" Jana asked. She didn't understand the situation the way Jeff did, but Jana was well aware that Danni came from a very painful background. It amazed Jana to see how happy Danni was, in spite of everything.

She had her moments, of course, and her stomach didn't handle stress well, but all in all, Danni was doing remarkably well. It made Jana want to investigate more about the faith that Danni and Jeff shared in Jesus. Jana wasn't ready to commit yet, but she was beginning to come around, which pleased her friends to no end.

"No," Danni replied. "I've tried to talk to her several times, but she refuses to even listen to me. She just makes nasty remarks about 'that boy' and then finally hangs up on me. I don't understand her."

Jana patted her hand, and they lost themselves in the fabric swatches. They laughed and chatted easily for several hours. Jana declared that she would never get married unless Jeff suddenly announced that he had a long-lost brother.

16

Meanwhile, Jeff had realized that he had forgotten a file he needed at work, so he ran to pick it up and was on the way back to the lake house. He was determined to do a superior job on the advertising campaign. Jeff loved his new job but couldn't wait to see Danni. His thoughts were on her, and he was thanking God again for meeting her as he maneuvered his Porsche around the surprisingly sharp curves leading to the driveway of the lake house. He still couldn't believe they would be married in just a few weeks.

A huge thunderstorm that had been rumbling and threatening for several hours finally broke and split the sky. It was loud and ferocious, especially for this time of year. That, and given that it had just grown dark, made the driving very tricky.

Jeff never saw the other car until it was too late. It all happened so fast. With a turn of the steering wheel, the driver of the other car nearly plowed into Jeff's car. The other driver went completely into his lane and almost hit him head-on. Thanks to the illumination from the headlights, and the ferocious lightning, Jeff got a good look at the driver's face and tried to cut the wheel too sharply to avoid hitting the other car.

Jeff turned it too much, too quickly. The car skidded and flipped over endlessly as it crashed down the steep embankment, taking out several large trees and rocks on the way down. It slammed into the deep, churning lake far below. The storm made it nearly impossible to see his car hit the water.

The driver of the other car never stopped but did call 9-1-1 to report an accident. The caller's voice was totally flat and devoid of any emotion. He quickly fled the scene as flames shot up and Jeff's car exploded.

Danni was getting worried. It was way past time for Jeff to arrive. He was always on time, or more often than not, early, for their plans. This was totally unlike him. "I don't get it, Jana. Something feels wrong," Danni said, pacing. "The answering machine keeps picking up at his house and office. I can't even get through on his cell phone."

Jana looked up from the pamphlets and samples on the table. "Danni, let's be realistic here. He's such a romantic, he's probably out buying you some flowers or candy or a puppy."

By the time he was three hours late, Danni was crying, and even Jana was worried.

A few minutes later, a forceful knock broke the silence. Danni nearly tripped over her long legs answering it. Two severe-looking police officers were crowded in the doorway. They were unsmiling. "We are looking for Danielle Graden," the larger of the two men said.

"That's me," Danni said, shrinking back and beginning to tremble.

"Do you know Jeffrey Kingston?"

"Yes...he's my fiancé," Danni replied.

"We regret to inform you that he was killed in a car accident earlier this evening."

"No!" Danni screamed, doubled over, and fell to her knees, sobbing. It was a primal sound of pain from the deepest part of her heart.

Jana, who had been standing right behind her, tried to comfort her. The officers helped Jana get Danni to the sofa. This was the part of their work they hated the most. It never got any easier.

"He's not dead," Danni said weakly. "He's coming to get us. We're getting married in four weeks." Danni shook her head slowly to either numb her senses or clear them, she wasn't sure which. Nothing made any sense.

"What happened?" Jana asked.

The older officer explained, "Apparently, it looks like Mr. Kingston wrecked his car in order to avoid being hit by a driver who crossed into his lane. The other car may have been speeding, and he didn't have time to do much about it. He lost control when he turned too sharply and then flipped down an embankment. The car exploded and slipped into the water." The officer put a hand on Danni's shoulder as she sobbed uncontrollably.

"Oh, God, please bring him back. Please," she prayed. She tried to stand up but just couldn't. The room tilted at a lop-sided angle, and she got dizzy. Everything was spinning. Somewhere in the distance, Danni could hear the voices and Jana and the police officers. She didn't know exactly where they were coming from, and she didn't care. All she cared about was Jeff.

"I think she will be fine," the doctor said as Danni lay still in the hospital bed. "Sometimes, family and friends of loved ones go into a state of shock after a death, especially if it is sudden." Danni stirred and whispered Jeff's name. The doctor shook his head and replaced her chart before nodding to Jana.

"I will keep a close eye on her," Jana promised with a worried frown. The two police officers had helped Jana get Danni to the hospital before they had to go answer another call. And so it went. Jana didn't envy them their job. It was going to be hard enough to help Danni pick up the pieces. She couldn't imagine having to deliver such horrible news to people on a regular basis.

When she woke up an hour later, Danni asked, "Where's Jeff? I dreamed he was hurt." Danni's eyes looked huge and haunted.

Jana patted her hand. "Danni, Jeff was in an accident. He's not coming back." As she said the words, Jana felt sick to her stomach. She was in pain for Danni, and her heart hurt. Jeff was like a brother to her. His sudden death was a tragedy of epic proportions. In a moment, everything had changed.

Danni sobbed. There was no hiding from the truth. Death had taken away someone else she dearly loved. This time, it was the one she loved most of all. The beautiful diamond ring sparkled under the harsh lights of the sterile hospital room. Fresh tears rolled down her face as Danni looked at it, remembering the day they had gotten engaged on the hot air balloon ride.

A short time later, Jana took Danni home and called LaMika. She rushed over, and they took turns crying and talking and feeling like all their lives had just been blown apart. Mercifully, the doctor at the hospital had given Danni some medication to help her rest.

Danni woke up when the medication wore off and insisted on calling Rachel and Connor herself. It was the worst phone call she could ever imagine having to make. It tore out her heart. Connor had to rush Rachel to the hospital when she began having chest pains.

Danni didn't even think of calling her own family until the next morning. They brought her no love, no comfort. Danni was all alone now. She slept fitfully for a short time, woke up, cried, and started the process over again. She had never forgotten Beth, but she remembered her now more than ever.

Now Jeff was gone too. Shattered were their dreams—all of the things they wanted to do, always together. The places they would travel, the babies and pets they would have, all they wanted to do. They had even been planning a mission trip together. Now it was all over. Gone. Forever. Just like that.

Jana and LaMika decided to make camp at Danni's apartment for as long as she needed them. They both wondered if Danni would be able to survive the loss of Jeff. He was one of those larger-than-life, real-life heroes, the kind of person who comes along once-in-a-lifetime if you are really blessed. Danni was certainly blessed, and now he was gone with no warning. They loved each other so much that it made people feel good just to be around them. Now everything had changed.

Jana took it upon herself to call Danni's family. Even though she'd only met them a few times, Jana really didn't like them. They made her skin crawl, and Jana could never understand how Danni came from that family.

Iris said she was very sorry to hear about Jeff and said all the appropriate things, but Jana felt cold talking to her. Danni's whole family felt so uncaring to Jana. Iris said to let her know when the services would be held, and they would attend, and then take their baby back home with them. Jana almost told her there was no way she would let them take Danni back to Mountainview, but she was mercifully able to bite her tongue.

Later the next morning, Danni emerged from her room, looking red-eyed and haggard. Her usually impeccable appearance was terrible. She had fallen asleep in one of Jeff's old shirts. Her makeup was streaked all over her face, and her long hair was all tangled. Without saying a word, LaMika and Jana hugged her and got her a cup of hot tea.

Danni was there physically but not really there in her spirit. Nothing felt right. She was utterly broken, and her stomach hurt more than it ever had in her life. Danni couldn't believe her heart was still beating.

Danni spoke briefly with Connor and Rachel, and they

agreed to have the funeral in Charlotte. Jana and LaMika rushed in to help with the details. It was odd to think there would be no body to bury. Danni had cried copiously when she realized that.

The funeral was to be held in their church, the same one they had attended together all through their college years, the same church where they were to have been married. Never again would they walk in together.

Iris called a few times before the service, but Jana screened all the calls. She was determined to spare Danni from facing as much unpleasantness as possible. Just breathing from one moment to the next was enough of a challenge.

On the morning of the funeral, Danni felt a hundred years old and looked as if she would faint any minute. She moved woodenly as she dressed in black, from head to toe. Her eyes saw nothing through the tears. She only heard Jeff's voice saying, "I love you" to her in her head.

17

The service was small and private. Only Jeff's closest friends joined Danni, Connor, and Rachel, along with Iris and Kurt. The only ones who weren't moved by the service were Iris and Kurt. Ruby hadn't bothered to attend, but Danni never noticed. Kurt had wanted to give Danni some money instead of attending the service, but Iris had insisted that it would look bad if he did that. Kurt had agreed, and they sneaked in just as the service was beginning and sat on the back row.

Danni sat between Connor and Rachel, who gripped her hands tightly the whole time. They looked as pale and unhappy as Danni. Several times during the service, Danni felt her heart beating in her ears and the room began so spin. Somehow, she decided, by sheer force of will, that it would have dishonored Jeff if she fainted, so she held on. She knew he needed her to be strong, as did Connor and Rachel. She surprised herself that she was still holding it together, albeit just barely.

Danni rode to the cemetery with the Kingstons. Jana, La-Mika, Steve, Matt, and Derrick stood close to them as the minister said a few final words. He seemed to talk forever. He prayed, and Danni wanted to cry out that it was all wrong and a horrible mistake. Jeff wasn't dead, she thought. He would come walking up any minute and say that it had all been a terrible mix-up. But he never came, and he never would.

After the minister's prayer, Danni walked over and placed a single white rose on the empty coffin. A part of her died with

Jeff. Rachel swayed and almost fainted, and Connor didn't look much better.

Rachel revived a bit and pulled Danni close. "You know we love you, Danni. Please stay in touch. Come and see us anytime. Please." The three of them cried and clung to each other. Connor was anxious to get Rachel home and have their trusted family physician take care of her.

Connor tearfully added, "Please don't hesitate if you ever need anything."

Connor and Rachel looked so heartbroken that Danni didn't know what to say. All she could do was cry and nod. Connor and Rachel Kingston looked exactly like Linda and Daniel Bradley had when they buried Beth.

While the others were paying their respects to Connor and Rachel, Iris and Kurt approached Danni. Danni noticed that they were both dressed in bright, festive colors like they had something to celebrate.

"Well, now that this mess is over, you can come home with us," Iris said dismissively as she picked an imaginary piece of lint from her dress.

"No!" Danni almost shrieked. There was absolutely no way she would ever go back there again. She had avoided it for the better part of almost four years, and she didn't intend to fall back into that nightmare again.

"I beg your pardon," Kurt said indignantly. "It would only look proper if you returned with us." He shifted from one foot to the other and snorted like a spirited stallion ready to bolt through a gate.

"I just lost the man I love, and I need to be here with my friends and my work to try and keep my mind off it, as much as I can," Danni nearly spat the words at them.

Iris and Kurt were both clearly angry. "Well, I can see that you are being overly dramatic again," Iris said. "Call us when you have come to your senses." With that, they turned and left. No hugs, no words of comfort, nothing.

The next few days passed in a jumble of nightmares and tears. When she had used up all of her allotted sick days, Danni returned to school. Her students, who were usually good, were better than ever, mercifully.

Her supervising teacher was very understanding, as was Dr. Gwent. Dr. Gwent had called several times to make sure Danni was okay. Jana had kept Dr. Gwent informed of Danni's condition. Because Dr. Gwent meant so much to Danni, she had made sure Jeff met him. Dr. Gwent had wholeheartedly approved of him and was stunned by his death.

Danni still felt numb, like she was sleepwalking through life. She picked up a painting Jeff had bought her during one of their visits to see Connor and Rachel in Chicago. It was a silly piece that featured a frog sitting on the back of a unicorn. The significance was something only the two of them would have understood. They were so close they shared an unspoken language, and now she was the only one left who could speak it. It was all too much. She picked up the painting and slammed it as hard as she could against her bedroom wall. The glass shattered into tiny pieces, just like her heart. It hit the floor, and she slid down onto the floor and cried until she had no tears left. Danni slept there that night.

"How could You take him from me?" Danni screamed into the darkness.

By the end of the next week, Danni was able to pour her heart out to God. She had been in such a state of shock that she shut down and had been on autopilot. Now she screamed and railed at God and cried more than she ever thought possible. She begged Him to forgive her for her anger and harsh words, and now she asked Him to just carry her through this nightmare, moment by moment.

She finally felt ready to go back to volunteering at the mission, something she dearly loved. Now that she didn't have Jeff around anymore, her schedule had opened up. She suddenly had a lot of empty hours to fill. Danni felt like she had nothing but time now. She soon found herself staying late each time she volunteered at the mission.

Sweet Jake, the beloved face of the mission, the mentor who'd first challenged and encouraged Danni to boldly share her faith, had died two years ago in his sleep. Two years after Jake's death, it was still sad to realize he wouldn't be there, but she knew that he was partying in heaven with Jeff. One day she would join them too. On her second night back since Jeff's death, Danni looked around for Carla. She was hoping to see her, but she never came in.

Danni helped close down the mission for the night and then walked to her beloved Mercedes. She had just put the key in the lock when someone called her name. Danni had parked in the alley, which had always made her uncomfortable, but it was what it was.

"Who's there?" Danni asked. It was dark, and the alley was poorly lit.

"It's Carla," came the weak reply.

"Where are you?" Danni asked, looking around nervously.

"I'm over by the trash cans."

Danni nervously approached and called out to Carla. Just then, she heard what sounded like a tiny cat mewing. She looked around the side of the dumpster and saw Carla, all bundled up against the cold, once again looking like she was wearing every single piece of clothing she owned.

Danni's eyes widened as she caught sight of a squirming bundle in Carla's arms. "Carla, what happened?" Danni asked, but she already knew.

"I just had a baby. It's a boy," she said weakly.

"Here, let me get you to a hospital. We need to make sure you're both okay," Danni offered.

"No, no. Don't. Please, just take the baby," Carla implored.

"What? Take your baby? Carla, I can't do that," Danni said.

"You have to, Danni. You just have to. I don't have anybody else, and you're the only person I can trust. Take him, please. Harvey is crazy. This is my one chance to get my baby away from him. You know he beats me. He was so mad when he found out I was pregnant. Please, please help me. I don't have much time. Please say you'll help me," Carla cried.

Danni had never seen anyone in such a state. She reached out her arms and took the baby when Carla handed him to her.

"He's the only good thing I've ever done in my life. Please take care of him, and don't let Harvey get him."

"What will you tell Harvey?" Danni asked as she unconsciously began rocking him gently back and forth.

"I'll tell him it was stillborn, and that will be that. He'll be glad," Carla said sadly as she got to her feet. "Promise me you will take care of him, Danni. Please."

"I will," Danni said. Before Danni could say anything else, Carla was gone. She was alone with the tiny baby, who was wrinkled and adorable, and she knew she had to get him out of the cold.

Danni hurried to her car and realized she didn't have a baby seat or anything he would need. She was totally unprepared for this. She secured him to the best of her ability and drove to the nearest store that sold baby gear. She got the basics, including diapers, wipes, clothes, and a car seat, and hurried back to her apartment.

Upon examination, it was clear the baby was no more than a few hours old. Danni knew she would have to take him to the hospital the next day and contact social services. She winced as she remembered her promise to Carla. She spent most of the night up with the baby and got him fed and bathed and dressed in some warm clothes she'd bought.

The next morning, Danni turned on the news and was stunned to see a photo of Carla. She turned up the volume as the announcer said, "This local homeless woman was found dead last night. It appears that she overdosed on drugs and then fell into a fire that was burning to keep members of a local homeless encampment warm..."

A chill ran down Danni's spine. It was no accident. Carla didn't do drugs. Danni knew with every fiber of her being that Harvey had done this to her. She now realized the baby was hers, for better or for worse. And as she looked at the little guy, dozing peacefully in the bassinet she had bought, she knew he was a blessing. Danni got down on her knees, right then and there, and prayed over him. She asked God to guide, guard, direct, and protect both of them.

She didn't know if she was still so muddled over losing Jeff, or if it was really God speaking to her, but she was filled with an enormous sense of both peace and purpose as she finished her prayer. The baby was beautiful. He had big blue eyes and dark hair and fair skin. She decided to name him Blake Jeffrey Graden. She had no idea how she was going to explain things, but with Harvey still on the loose and remembering how Carla had often said he had "connections to people in high places," she didn't want to risk telling anyone about how he came to be in her care.

Within two days, Danni had taken Blake to a pediatrician, gotten him all checked out, and set up in her apartment. She then made an appointment to see Dr. Gwent to try to explain things to him. When she walked in, he was clearly stunned to see Blake with her in his little carrier. She had vowed to keep her promise to Carla no matter what.

When she left Dr. Gwent's office an hour later, she was shell-shocked. She had lost her teaching credentials. Because of the morals contract with her scholarship, she couldn't be an unwed mother. So, she had lost her scholarship and would have to pay the scholarship committee back. She wouldn't be a teacher, after all. But there was no way she was going to tell anyone how Blake came to be hers. Danni knew she just couldn't take the risk of losing him.

Jana and LaMika were both shocked when she introduced them to Blake. They both believed he was somehow Jeff's son. Danni said he wasn't, and begged them both to "just trust her." It was awkward for sure. They trusted Danni but were still stunned.

Within a few more days, Danni found a job at a local newspaper. The pay was good. It wasn't stellar, but it was good. She sold her wedding dress and engagement ring. It nearly tore her heart out to do so, but she knew that Jeff would understand.

Little Blake Jeffrey quickly became the apple of his mommy's eye. She cried when she sold her car, but it brought in a nice price and added a bit of a cushion to Danni's bank account. She bought an ugly but very safe and reliable station wagon that perfectly suited her needs.

Pretty soon, Danni lost touch with almost all of her old friends, except Jana and LaMika. She didn't really care, though. She was totally wrapped up in her baby, who meant the world to her.

Iris had demanded to know why Danni wouldn't come home. Danni took pleasure in telling her it was because she had a baby to take care of. The stream of obscenities Iris let flow was just embarrassing. She told Danni to "give it up for adoption so she didn't embarrass her father's good name," and Danni just laughed and slammed down the phone. Iris still called from time to time but never asked about the baby, and Danni just didn't care anymore.

18

Danni got a long and loving letter from Connor and Rachel saying they were going to Europe for an "extended sabbatical." They had learned that Rachel had advanced heart disease, and the stress of losing Jeff had almost sent her over the edge. They felt a change of scenery would help them both. At the close of the letter, they assured her of their love for her, of which she had no doubt. But it was still sad. It was like losing her last connection to Jeff.

Sometimes, when she was taking care of little Blake, Danni let herself pretend, for just a moment, that Jeff was still alive, they were married, and Blake was theirs. What a sweet dream that was. But she didn't let herself linger there, or the fall would have been too painful. Little by little, Danni was beginning to accept that Jeff was gone, and she knew there would never be another man who could claim her heart the way he had.

Blake was an absolute joy. Despite their initial questions, LaMika and Jana became doting "aunts" to him. He was the best baby Danni could have ever dreamed of. He rarely cried and was always in a good humor. He had the cutest little giggle.

As Blake grew, his dark hair curled up, and he drooled a lot. Blake went everywhere with Danni. She was thankful to be able to work from home most of the time. When she had to go to the office, Blake went too. As he got bigger, Blake discovered his toes and spent a lot of time playing with them. And, with everything he did, Danni declared he was "the smartest baby ever!"

By the time he was ten months old, Blake was just about ready to walk. He began cruising around, holding onto furniture, and Danni knew it was just a matter of time before he was into everything. His first word was "Mommy" and that pleased Danni to no end. Mercifully too, Blake and her job kept Danni busy. He looked enough like Danni to pass as her biological son. She didn't care what he looked like. He was her whole world.

The only time she was lonely was late at night, long after Blake was asleep in his crib. Then, beautiful memories of Jeff crept in. She often wondered why it had happened. It was so hard not to be angry. But then she looked at her son, and she knew that God still loved her and had a plan for her life. She was so thankful for that truth.

Just like so many other people, the folks at the church she'd attended with Jeff thought the baby was theirs. There had been too many looks and questions, and it was just easier for her to find another church. She found a good, Bible-believing, Bible-preaching church not too far from her apartment.

This time was easier because she and Blake went as a package deal. It was easier to let them think she was single mom, which she actually was. There was no Jeff to go with her now. He was with Jesus; he didn't need to go to church any longer.

Danni had to do some work in the office on a hot afternoon just a few days after one of their treasured trips to the park with Aunt Jana and Aunt LaMika. Blake was unusually cranky and refused to play with any of his favorite toys. Danni kept a "busy bag" in her desk drawer for his visits, but today he was having none of it.

Each time she handed him a toy, he yelled, "No!" and threw it down. All of her begging and pleading didn't work. By early evening, he was crying loudly and rubbing his eyes. Danni checked his forehead, which was beginning to feel warm. She put him down in his crib and went to get the thermometer.

When she returned a short time later, he began vomiting and crying, which made him throw up again. By the time she cleaned up the mess, she decided to run a bath for him and contact the doctor's on-call service. She was worried.

By the time there was the right amount of water in the tub, Danni put Blake in, and his nose began bleeding. It started out as a trickle and soon bled more and more, faster and faster. Danni tried in vain to stop the bleeding while Blake was screaming and throwing up again.

Danni grabbed her purse, diaper bag, and keys and rushed downstairs with Blake. She left her door open, and a kindly old neighbor heard the commotion. She turned off the tub and cleaned it up before any damage happened.

Danni drove as fast as possible to the hospital, dodging traffic like a runaway train. It was a miracle the police didn't stop her. But she wouldn't have stopped anyway. The only thing she could think of was her child. Blake was almost unconscious now. He was a bluish-gray, and it tore Danni's heart out. She had to fight to keep her nerves in check and the tears from blurring her vision as she drove.

She careened around the corner into the hospital parking lot and halted in front of the emergency room entrance. She grabbed Blake and rushed inside. A nurse and two orderlies approached her and saw she was a mother with a very sick child. Someone laid Blake on a stretcher, and he was quickly whisked away.

A nurse grabbed a chart, and Danni supplied the information to the best of her ability as she tried to chase after Blake. The kind nurse stopped her at a set of metal double doors. It wasn't until much later that Danni noticed the blood on the front of her shirt. It was actually one of Jeff's old shirts, which just made her miss him even more.

A short time later, another nurse approached Danni. She put a hand on her shoulder and asked, "Is there anyone I can call for you? I don't want you to be alone right now."

Danni had never felt more alone in her life. She gave her LaMika and Jana's numbers. The nurse called them, and they both rushed over.

"This is all my fault. I should have watched him more closely or seen that he was getting sick," Danni said between sobs.

"Now, I don't want any more of this foolish talk. You're the best little mama I've ever known," LaMika said as she patted Danni's hand, and Jana agreed. LaMika was worried but tried her best not to show it. From what Danni had told her, things sounded very serious. LaMika quietly excused herself and went to see if she could ferret out some more information. Jana sat quietly with Danni, not knowing exactly what to say.

A short time later, LaMika returned, followed closely by a grim-faced Dr. Patterson. Blake's own pediatrician was out of town on holiday. LaMika was relieved to see that at least a seasoned replacement had been found. Although she worked at a different hospital, every medical professional in the area knew about and respected Dr. Patterson.

"Ms. Graden?" The doctor nodded curtly to her. He immediately said, "We are doing all we can for Blake. He's a very sick little boy. It is most definitely a serious situation. We are running a complete series of tests on him. We should have the results in a few hours."

"Serious situation?" Danni croaked, stunned. Just yesterday, he had been playing "Big Baby Rabbit" with her. Now he was in serious condition.

"I'm afraid I can't give you anything more definitive for a few more hours. I will let you know as soon as we have the results." He excused himself and disappeared behind the foreboding double doors.

Danni periodically tried to peek through the doors but always saw nothing. When she had asked to see Blake earlier, she got a firm, "No!" and that was that.

Three grueling hours later, Dr. Patterson returned. "We have the results now," he said.

Danni mentally tried to brace herself for the coming onslaught. "What? What is wrong with my son?" she asked.

"There is no easy way to say this, but your son has a very rare form of bone cancer. I'm afraid it began to spread through his body shortly after his birth, slowly at first and then at a more rapid pace.

"Oh, dear Lord, help us. What does that mean?" Danni asked.

The doctor explained the technical aspects of the situation. Afterward, he said, "Blake is a very sick little boy. It is imperative that we find a donor for him immediately. This condition is fatal far more quickly in young children." The doctor then excused himself to check on his young patient, leaving Danni to absorb the news with LaMika and Jana.

Danni ran to the bathroom to be sick. She was violently ill and then felt sick again.

Once she came out of the bathroom, LaMika and Jana were hovering near the door. "Are you okay?" LaMika and Jana asked, in unison.

"No, but I will be as soon as I find Blake a donor." She knew it had to be a blood relative but felt compelled to try anyway. So, she, LaMika, and Jana all tried, but none were a match. Danni was allowed to visit Blake briefly. He was sedated and didn't know she was there, but she prayed over him and kissed him. He finally opened his eyes and said, "Mommy," and then drifted off to sleep again.

Danni took a deep breath, marched out to meet Jana and LaMika, and told them how Blake came to be her son. They were flabbergasted. "I have nothing to lose now. I don't care what happens as long as I save my son," she said. "Will you two please stay with him? I've got to get to Arkansas and see if I can find a relative. I've kept tabs on Harvey through my connections at work. He died in a bar fight and doesn't seem to have any relatives. I was always afraid somehow one of them would find me and take Blake away. I know it sounds weird now, but it always worried me. Carla's mom and her aunt are still alive. Maybe if I appeal to them, they will listen."

Jana and LaMika readily agreed, and Danni took off as fast as she could go. She kept a change of clothes in the station wagon in case Blake had a mishap on her, so she changed quickly at the airport and got a ticket to Arkansas. By the grace of God, she was in Little Rock in a matter of hours.

She found Carla's mom and aunt, who shared an apartment. It took Danni about three seconds to understand why Carla had run away, but at that point, Danni didn't care. She didn't give them much of a choice. She hauled both of the intoxicated women to her rental car and drove them to the nearest hospital, where they both got tested.

Danni returned them to their filthy apartment and told them if either was a match, she would let them know. The idea of them refusing to help was not an acceptable option.

Danni hurried back to the airport. All she could think of was getting back to her baby. She had to take two connecting flights to get home, but thankfully, there were no delays or long layovers. She was back at the hospital in almost record time.

But her nerves were frazzled, and her stomach was raging inside her. "Any news?" she asked worriedly as she saw LaMika.

"No, honey. He's been asleep almost the whole time you were gone. Jana is sitting with him now. How was Arkansas?" LaMika asked as she hugged Danni.

"I took them both to be tested to see if either is a match for Blake. Hopefully, we'll get some good news soon," Danni replied, anxious to go see her baby.

But the news wasn't good. Neither Carla's mom nor her aunt turned out to be a match for Blake. His condition was worsening by the minute.

Danni stayed either by Blake's bedside or in the waiting room. LaMika and Jana tag-teamed each other so she didn't have to spend too much time alone.

A week later, for what felt like the thousandth time, Danni slipped quietly into Blake's room. Silent tears rolled in rivers down her cheeks as she looked around the room. His favorite toys were positioned nearby, but he was too sick to play with them.

Blake, who had been sleeping, opened his eyes and said, "Mommy, wuv wu."

She had been holding his hand, and Blake squeezed her hand. The room got so still and so quiet and peaceful. A blanket of peace and soft light seemed to fill the whole room.

"No!" Danni screamed as she clutched him to her, knowing it was already too late. He was gone now. There was nothing she could do.

Doctors, nurses, and other attendants rushed into the room. Someone shoved Danni out of the way as she sobbed helplessly in the doorway. They worked furiously to save him, but it was too late. Little Blake Jeffrey Graden was now in heaven.

Danni never understood how she was able to hold up, but she did. God made a way. She picked out his little casket, her favorite outfit of his, and his favorite stuffed animal. She thanked people, nodded politely, and got through the funeral. Danni had Blake buried beside Jeff. It seemed fitting somehow.

The two people she had loved most in this life were now gone. But she knew they weren't really gone. The love would live in her heart, and she would see them in heaven someday. It was just the "until then" part that broke her heart into a million pieces.

Even though Jeff was gone, he had blessed her again. Exactly three days after Blake's funeral, the medical bills started rolling in. But thanks to the stunning engagement ring, the car, and even some rare art pieces Jeff had given her, Danni was able to pay off the bills and put that part of her life behind her. She had also been able to pay the "early release" from her scholarship, and she was eternally thankful for that.

Danni couldn't bear the apartment without Blake, so she moved to a different apartment and kept working. All she did was exist. She surprised herself when she kept waking up every day. She had thought that someone with a broken heart would die, but she kept waking up, day after day.

19

About six months later, Danni was so exhausted and stressed that she decided to finally take a Saturday off. She went to a movie and then did a little shopping. She was exiting one of her long-forgotten favorite stores when the wind began whipping her long beautiful mane around her face. Momentarily distracted, she didn't see the handsome gentleman coming from the opposite direction until she collided with him, nearly knocking them both to the ground.

"I'm sorry," Danni said. Once she regained her balance and composure, she stretched up to her full height and looked at the man. "I'm so sorry. I beg your pardon," Danni said. "I think I need to look where I am going." She was able to almost look the stranger in the eye. He was tall and lean, with handsome features. His olive skin, dark eyes, and dark, wavy hair gave him an exotic air.

The man was instantly impressed by Danni. He had rarely seen a woman so tall, so beautiful, and so completely unassuming. And, in his business, beautiful people were the norm instead of the exception. He thought her features were both delicate and striking at the same time. And he couldn't help noticing the deep sadness in her eyes.

"I beg your pardon," he said, remembering his good manners and fine upbringing. "It is I who needs to look where I am going so I won't be knocked over by beautiful ladies. But, on second thought..." He smiled and looked very youthful, although Danni guessed he had to be older than she was. "My name is Aristotle Zambini."

"I'm Danni Graden."

They chatted for a few minutes, and then he surprised her by asking, "Danni, where do you work?"

"I write for the *Charlotte Sun Chronicle*." Something about the way he said it made her faintly uneasy. She wasn't afraid of him, but she had the distinct feeling he was appraising her, and her self-esteem wasn't too high.

"I run a fashion house in New York, and I would love to help you put a portfolio together, if you don't already have one. With your looks and personality, you could take the fashion world by storm." He gave her a genuine smile and handed her a card. He hastily scribbled down the name of the hotel where he was staying locally. "I'm here on business until Monday. Please think it over. If you decide to 'go for it,' as you Americans say, then give me a call."

He bade her goodbye and was gone, leaving Danni stunned. She stared at the card for a moment. It included the address, phone number, email, and fax number for a location in New York City. It was embossed in heavy gold lettering on a thickly textured white card. It was obviously expensive.

Danni looked at it once more, then shoved it into the pocket of her red coat. As she drove back to her lonely apartment, Danni pushed the idea of Aristotle Zambini out of her mind. It was ridiculous.

The next day, Danni overslept and didn't hear her alarm clock, which meant she completely missed church services, something she rarely did. She had her morning devotion at the table with a cup of tea and a piece of toast. As she prayed, she asked God to guide her and help her with her loneliness. She came across Proverbs 3:5, which said, "Trust in the LORD with all thine heart; and lean not unto thine own understanding. In all thy ways acknowledge Him, and He shall direct thy paths."

She meditated and prayed on that truth for a long time; afterward, she didn't feel quite so lonely. Danni knew she would miss Jeff and Blake until the end of time, but knowing God wouldn't leave her gave her a feeling of comfort and peace that was her saving grace.

After Danni showered and got dressed, she decided to go into the office. When she arrived, the office wasn't very crowded, so she caught up on a few things and then decided to do a little research on Aristotle Zambini. She did a bit of hunting and found what she was looking for. There were tons of articles about Aristotle "Ari" Zambini and his fashion house. Aristotle was half-Greek, half-Italian. He and his parents had been very close. They traveled all over the world during his idyllic childhood. Unfortunately his parents were killed in a plane crash when Aristotle was fourteen. He was spared their fate because he was at home recovering from a bout with the flu.

After the death of his parents, he grew and flourished under the care of his Italian grandmother, who had a keen eye for fashion. By the age of twenty-one, he graduated from the Sorbonne, and a year later, with his grandmother's help, had founded his fashion house. Three years later, it expanded until he moved the headquarters to New York, and he had been there for twelve years.

Danni was pleased to read that he was a Christian and happily married to a former model from Hungary named Annuska. Apparently, he was known as the "George Washington of Fashion" for his forward-thinking and willingness to do anything he asked his people to do. He pushed himself harder than anyone.

Danni found article after article praising Aristotle Zambini for his genius. He was a maverick in the business. He was always a step ahead of the others in predicting the latest trends, colors, and fabrics. He somehow found the most beautiful, exotic, and often unique women and men to model for his fashion house. They wore his latest designs with an ease and flair second to none.

Danni was very impressed, to say the least, but couldn't understand why in the world Aristotle Zambini would want her. She finished her work and headed for home. It was so empty and quiet there with no voices and no laughter. The only noises came from Danni as she puttered around the apartment, trying to combat the stillness.

She thought about Jeff and Blake and Beth. She thought about Iris, whom she rarely spoke to anymore. Danni pondered calling LaMika or Jana. They were both such wonderful friends, but she felt like she was dragging them down. They were both busy, and even though they saw each other often, Danni felt like there was just a part of herself that wasn't there anymore. It was like standing in the middle of a crowded party where everyone was alive and happy and laughing, but you felt cold and alone.

Danni went to bed early and was having a hard time waking up the next morning after a very sweet dream about Jeff and Blake when the phone rang. She didn't want to wake up but knew she had to.

"May I speak to Miss Danni Graden?" a man asked politely.

"This is she," Danni said cautiously.

"This is Aristotle Zambini. You attacked me on the street two days ago," he said with a laugh, and Danni laughed too.

"Yes, I remember you, " Danni said. "How did you get my number?"

"Well, I was beginning to fear that I was not going to hear from you again. I wanted to talk with you one last time before I return to New York. If you join my group, you could make a fortune. This is going to be life-changing for you."

He was certainly persistent; Danni had to give him credit for that. He made her smile.

Ari continued, "If you agree, I can have a plane ticket delivered to you tomorrow. You will need to be in New York one week from today. Can you do that? Will you take a leap of faith?"

Danni only hesitated for a moment. Nothing was holding her here anymore, and there was no turning back now. "Yes, I can." Surprisingly, she felt relief at her decision, not fear. It served to show her that she had made the right decision.

"Yes!" Ari cheered on his end. He fist-pumped and just knew this was going to be the beginning of a long and illustrious journey for Danni. He chatted with her for a few more minutes and then hung up so he would make his plane on time. He couldn't wait to see his beloved Annuska and tell her all about the "Southern gem" he had just found.

Within a week, Danni had left her job, put her precious mementos from Jeff and Blake in storage, and given up her apartment. She gave her station wagon to the mission, which felt right. She packed her belongings into three suitcases and a small carry-on bag.

LaMika and Jana drove her to the airport. She hugged them both, and all three were crying. They had so much history among them, so many tears and prayers and memories. It felt like a lifetime in just a few years.

After one final hug and a fresh round of tears, Danni squared her shoulders and walked onto the plane. This was her second time flying without Jeff. Her first had been the frantic trip to Arkansas in a desperate attempt to find a donor for Blake. Now, she felt Jeff's heart-crushing loss all over again.

As the plane took off and reached its cruising altitude, Danni prayed and closed her eyes, trying to find rest. She was able to go to sleep, and the flight was smooth and uneventful. It was so different not having Jeff to lean on when she was nervous or afraid. Sometimes she still wondered if Jeff had lived could he have done something to help her save Blake's life.

She would never know the answer to that question, so all she could do was keep moving forward. Her Lancelot was lost to her forever, and Camelot was no more. That was her last thought as she drifted off to sleep for the remainder of the flight.

20

When the plane landed, Ari was waiting for Danni. "Hello, Danni. Welcome to New York. You look wonderful, by the way," he said. He kissed her on both cheeks and escorted her to the waiting black limousine. It startled her only momentarily since she had enjoyed many safe rides in limousines with Connor and Rachel over the years. She thought of Beth, but knew that everything was going to be okay.

Ari and Danni settled easily into a conversation about her flight, and he pointed out some of the wonderful sights as they made their way to her hotel. She tried not to gawk and look like a tourist, but it was difficult not to be impressed. The buildings were immense and seemed to stretch on forever in all directions. People and cars were moving everywhere at dizzying speeds. The city itself seemed to have a heartbeat and pulse that never stopped.

At last, they arrived at The Plaza. After getting her settled, Ari told Danni that the driver would pick her up at eight a.m. sharp, and she would meet him at the studio. Danni was thankful that Jeff, Connor, and Rachel had introduced her to this kind of lifestyle. It was definitely a far cry from life with the Gradens in Mountainview, North Carolina.

Danni ordered room service that night and sat cross-legged on the bed while she ate. She pulled the heavy velvet drapes back and enjoyed the twinkling lights of the skyline. It almost looked like a huge Christmas tree to her. She felt like a kid and grinned as she finished her meal and read her Bible before going to bed.

The next morning, Danni was downstairs and ready to roll fifteen minutes before the driver was scheduled to pick her up. She didn't want to be late. As promised, a gleaming gray Rolls pulled up at exactly eight o'clock, and she smiled happily as she slid inside. The driver maneuvered expertly in and out of the frantic traffic. The driver, a native New Yorker, had to grin as he looked back and saw the look of pure wonder on Danni's radiant face.

When they arrived at their destination, the driver deftly hopped out and assisted Danni. She was taken aback at the splendor of the building that lay before her. It was done in smoky glass with chrome features everywhere, and it looked starkly modern. It reached up to the sky like a wondrous tower among plain buildings. But the other buildings around it certainly weren't plain. It was just that the Zambini Building, like the man for whom it was named, was extraordinary and outshone them all.

As she entered the building, Danni noticed that the wonder didn't stop with the exterior. Black and white leather furniture, chrome fixtures, and huge mirrors were everywhere. With so many mirrors, Danni sure hoped she didn't have anything stuck in her teeth.

Ari Zambini clearly had an eye for decorating too. A receptionist nodded and welcomed her when she gave the woman her name. She pointed her to the bank of elevators. Danni noticed several impressive paintings and sculptures as she reached the elevators. Jeff and his dear family had introduced her to fine art, and she had a deep respect for it.

When she reached the top floor, she approached the secretary and gave her name. "Ah, Danni, we have heard so much about you, my dear. You are expected inside. Please go in," she said kindly.

Danni approached a set of double black doors that simply said, "A. Zambini." She pulled one open and walked inside.

Ari looked delighted to see her. He gave her a kiss on both cheeks and greeted her warmly. "Welcome, Danni. I'm so glad you're here."

"And I'm glad to be here, " Danni said, still in a bit of a daze. It was all so surreal to her.

He chatted amiably for a few moments and then buzzed for Anna, his secretary. "Tell Michael and Lauren we are ready," he said.

"Certainly, sir," came Anna's reply.

Ari rolled his eyes comically at the mention of "sir" but took it all in stride.

Danni laughed as Ari ushered her to his private elevator, and they rode down one floor. A tall, red-haired man named Michael greeted her, and then a tiny woman who looked like a Japanese princess introduced herself as Lauren. Danni liked them both immediately and soon figured out that Michael and Lauren were married.

Ari said, "Danni, Michael is the best stylist in the business, and Lauren's makeup work is second to none. It you will give them your permission, I want them to give you a new look—the Zambini look."

Although she was still overwhelmed by everything, Danni hadn't traveled all this way for nothing. She took a deep breath and said, "Let's go for it!"

Michael and Lauren both grinned, nodded to Ari, and ushered him out so they could get to work. They liked Danni a lot. She had none of the artifice or jading that most everyone in the business had, and it wasn't just because she was a newbie. There was definitely something very special about her.

Michael and Lauren went to work. They argued and planned

and then set about creating an entirely new look for Danni. By the time they were done, Danni was transformed from a small-town cutie to a full-blown glamour queen. Her nearly waist-length hair was really thick, so they layered it and cut off a few inches. Lauren said she couldn't believe Danni had ever battled acne. Her skin was practically flawless now. It made Danni unbelievably happy to hear her say that.

Lauren taught Danni all about accenting her high cheekbones and how to draw attention to her huge green eyes with eye shadow and mascara. Her heart-shaped face just begged to be loved by the camera, and Lauren and Michael were anxious to show Ari what they had done. They felt a bit like parents sending their beloved child off to her first day of school as they anxiously waited for Ari to come and see Danni.

Ari clapped his hands when he saw her. He hugged Danni and heartily congratulated Michael and Lauren. "Now for the clothes!" he said and whisked her off to wardrobe. They went to another floor, and it was like stepping into the closet of a fairy princess. There were people and mirrors and fabric and clothes and accessories everywhere.

Ari proudly introduced Danni to the love of his life, Annuska Zambini. Annuska was a striking redhead and extremely friendly. She hugged Danni as Ari introduced them. Although Ari was in charge of his design house, everyone knew that Annuska was his right hand in every way.

Annuska and Ari were crazy about each other. They both relished the grueling work and long hours it required to be at the top of their field and remain there. Although they got along well, their arguments could rattle the rooftops from time to time. They always made their peace quickly, and their work never suffered for it. In fact, it seemed to make it even better.

Although she was very good at what she did, Annuska knew

Ari just possessed a gift that no one else had, not even her. She was happy to be his muse and help him in any way she could. It worked well for them, and everyone who worked with them benefited from their combined creative genius.

Ari told Annuska that he thought the "magenta, number thirty-five" was perfect to start for Danni. Annuska agreed. Annuska took Danni by the hand, and Ari quickly disappeared.

Annuska led her through rows and rows and rows of exquisite clothing. The pieces were jaw-dropping to Danni. Annuska found the one Ari had suggested and pulled it out. It was a fabulous magenta velvet dress with a plunging neckline that was not scandalous. It was backless and looked simply stunning when Danni tried it on. She couldn't believe this was happening to her.

"Thank You, Lord," she whispered, smiling heavenward as she finished getting into the dress. "I know this was Your doing."

Once Danni was dressed, Annuska accompanied her back to Ari's office, carrying several more dresses that were just as beautiful as the one she was currently wearing.

The photographer who was going to be working with Danni was Brad Mitchell, an up-and-coming new star himself. He was chubby and had a fuzzy ponytail that made him look like a hippie, but he commanded authority. Brad clearly knew what he was doing. He had one of his assistants crank up the music, two others work on getting the lighting just right, and yet another get the props just so for him. In no time, Brad had Danni giving flirty looks, pouty looks, a serious face, and a few others by the time they were done.

Michael and Lauren were on hand to do any necessary touch-ups during the shoot. It was clear to everyone that the camera loved Danni, and a new star in the fashion world had just been born. They all sensed something truly special happening. Ari and Annuska quietly high-fived each other, and Annuska even did a little happy dance.

Annuska had been a bit skeptical when Ari had called her from Charlotte and told her he had just found "THE next modeling sensation" for their fashion house, but she could see now that her beloved husband had been exactly on point. Annuska just prayed that Danni would be happy with them.

By early evening, Danni thought she was going to drop from sheer exhaustion, but she didn't want to be a complainer. She was surprised to find out how much she liked modeling. Although she was just getting started, it was a lot of fun. She had always enjoyed clothes and putting outfits together, but this was a far cry from shopping at thrift stores on a very tight budget.

Once again, she was grateful to the Kingstons for introducing her to this kind of world. Otherwise, she would never have had the confidence to do it.

Finally, Brad announced that he was finished and turned on his heel and left without another word, leaving his people to disassemble everything. Ari and Annuska helped Danni gather her things. They both told her they were "very pleased" with how well things went, and Danni thanked them both profusely.

A driver was waiting to take Danni back to her hotel. She took a quick bath, put on some comfy clothes, and ordered room service. She barely had the energy to eat and read one chapter in her Bible before she fell asleep. This time, though, she didn't have any nightmares, which was a blessing.

Danni got to sleep in the next morning since Ari said she wouldn't be needed until the afternoon. She thought about writing Iris a letter but suspected that if she did, Iris would call her names and make fun of her for what she was doing. Her self-esteem was still shaky after all of the Gradens' abuse, so she decided it was best to put off writing to Iris, at least for now. Besides, if Ari was correct and Danni did make a splash in the fashion world, Iris would probably hear what Danni was up to, anyway.

Ari's prediction about Danni couldn't have been more accurate. Her portfolio from Brad Mitchell was beyond stunning. It proved that Danni was capable of a multitude of looks. Thanks to the tragedies in her life, she had a grounding and a substance that emanated from deep inside her, and the camera loved her for it. She was part girl-next-door and part glamour queen. Women wanted to be her, and men wanted to be next to her.

Danni became the toast of the Zambini Design House and all of New York in no time. Very quickly, the amount of money Danni earned was staggering. Three months later, she set up an anonymous scholarship fund in joint memory of Jeff and Blake. She wanted others to find a way out like she had. Only, maybe with this scholarship, the road out would be a bit less bumpy than Danni's was.

Danni was having the time of her life. She flew all over the country. She did work in Miami, Palm Beach, Los Angeles, Denver, and Hawaii. Photographers fell all over themselves to get a picture of her. Ari and Annuska guarded Danni fiercely. They loved her like family, and the feeling was mutual.

Ari and Annuska introduced Danni to another member of their design house. His name was Bryn Pateau, and he was their top male model. He looked a lot like a Ken doll come to life, with perfectly styled blonde hair, huge blue eyes, high cheekbones, and muscles that just went on for days. Bryn was so handsome that Danni was afraid if she looked directly at him, her eyeballs would melt. She had to admit he was quite a fox. He seemed totally unaware of his looks. He had been away for a time, but no one discussed it, so Danni didn't ask any questions.

21

Bryn and Danni hit it off immediately. "You are exquisite!" Bryn announced when he met Danni. He quickly kissed both of her hands and bowed extremely low, which broke the ice and made Danni laugh. Danni had been afraid that anyone who looked like Bryn would have been a snob, but nothing could have been further from the truth.

Ari and Annuska had been on a trip to Paris when they discovered Bryn, who was working on his parents' farm just outside the city. Ari and Annuska's car had broken down during a terrible storm, and they had happened upon the Pateaus' farm, desperately looking for help. The rest was history. Bryn never forgot where he came from and how blessed he was to be doing what he was doing. Ari and Annuska had led Bryn to Christ, and he was very thankful for that.

Bryn and Danni enjoyed Bible study together while they were on modeling trips. They both had a ridiculously goofy sense of humor, which kept the photoshoots lively. Although Danni did her best to keep in close touch with LaMika and Jana, it was a challenge with time and distance and travel. Bryn soon became Danni's best friend.

After Danni realized she truly loved what she was doing, Ari called her into his office. She was nervous, feeling like she was being called to the principal's office. She took a seat quietly.

"It's time for me to take you to Italy, if you want to go. This is the most important—"

"We're what?" Danni squealed, not even letting Ari finish his explanation. "Of course I want to go! Italy! Wow!" Danni clapped her hands excitedly, making Ari smile. She was so innocent, despite the worldliness around her. He was thankful for her foundation in Christ. Ari wisely knew it would be a blessing to her in more ways than she could have realized.

The conversation was interrupted when Anna buzzed in and said that Bryn had arrived. He strolled in, shook hands warmly with Ari, and kissed both of Danni's cheeks.

Bryn smiled excitedly as he sat beside Danni, and Ari shared the news with him. He was thrilled that his best friend was going with him. It would be their first international trip together. Danni spoke French well, and she enjoyed speaking to Bryn in his native language.

Although Bryn spoke English very well, he still got things mixed up a bit from time to time, and it endeared him to Danni. Plus, it provided more fodder for her to good-naturedly tease him, and they both loved to laugh.

That night, Danni twirled around with a huge smile on her face when she went back to her new loft apartment. Ari and Annuska's real estate agent had helped her find it, and Bryn helped her get moved in. It looked a bit like the Zambini Design House, only on a much, much smaller scale.

Sleek, black leather furniture dominated the apartment, and modern glass tables adorned the living room and dining area. The kitchen was filled with sleek stainless steel appliances, and the floors were covered in black and white tile. A view of the New York City skyline was evident when she pulled back the heavy black and white drapes that hid her from the rest of the world. She didn't hide quite as much anymore, and the pain had lessened, but it was still there.

She had accepted that Jeff and Blake were gone, but the love remained. Danni knew the love would be with her forever. Sometimes a wave of grief washed over her, so sharp and so fresh that it took her breath away. At other times, she had trouble remembering certain details about them. At those times, the guilt plagued her—she was alive, and they weren't.

Danni made a point of staying connected to God with her prayer and Bible time, no matter where she was. She never forgot throwing the ridiculous picture of the frog and the unicorn and how it shattered, and how angry she had been at God. Danni didn't ever want to go back to such a dark time ever again.

Danni packed for the trip to Italy and carefully wrapped small photos of Jeff and Blake and put them at the very bottom of her suitcase. "I love you both," she whispered as she zipped it shut, turned out the light, and twin tears slid down her cheeks.

22

The flight was a wonderful experience. Ari, Annuska, Danni, Bryn, Michael, Lauren, two other models, and three of Ari's favorite photographers hopped onto Ari and Annuska's private plane. They enjoyed some champagne and tasty food. It was a festive, celebratory atmosphere. Danni had read several books about Italy to get prepared.

Bryn generously shared some of his travel experiences with her, and Ari spoke of his family's Italian heritage with great fondness. Danni hoped she was ready for this new path her life was taking her on. Danni often felt like she could not regain her balance before life began to dip and turn like a roller coaster, over and over.

When they landed at the Leonardo da Vinci Airport in the impressive southwest region of Rome, Danni bounded off the plane with a robust spirit. Her long, luxurious mane flapped in the breeze. She was wearing a long, red dress with a slit up the front and a matching straw hat that she had to clutch so it didn't blow off her head. Danni's oversized tortoise shell sunglasses made her look elegant and mysterious. Ari and Annuska were both pleased with her.

Ari looked dashing in a crisp linen suit that perfectly enhanced his dark skin. The others were fashionably dressed, as always, in something from the design house. Ari expected anyone and everyone associated with his design house to dress well at all times and in his clothes, of course. He had a temper, and he worked hard, but he had a huge, kind heart and would do anything possible to help others.

His and Annuska's one heartbreak was they had not been able to have children. Doctors had not been able to find out why. Although they were open to adoption, they were still holding out hope for a biological child. But, until then, their design house and all of its people were their "babies," and they couldn't have been prouder.

Ari gathered his people around as the last of them exited the jet. He and the others waved to the Italian press, who had converged for a photo opportunity. Gorgeous photos of Danni and Bryn were all over the front page of the next edition of *Il Messagero.* They looked tall and beautiful and carefree. No one who didn't know her would have ever guessed that Danni had been scared to death and wondering where her trusty bottle of Pepto Bismol was.

"Buon giorno, Signora," the driver said as she entered the waiting limo. The others divided up and piled into the limos standing by to whisk them through the streets of Rome. Bryn slid easily in beside Danni. It reminded Danni a bit of New York, but with its own definitive vibe. They got stuck in a traffic jam, and she could hear the blaring horns of impatient and hurried drivers all around her. But this time, she heard insults being hurled around in Italian, and she couldn't understand a lot of what was being said.

Although there were many tall buildings forming an impressive skyline, it didn't have the cramped and jammed feel of New York. It seemed like a whole other world. And it was. The buildings were made of stone in various forms of Corinthian and Classical Roman architectural styles. They were impressive structures. None were dirty and smog-laden the way they were in New York. Rome was a city that was well-tended and greatly loved. Not that

New York wasn't; it was just different, and Danni appreciated both. As she gazed out the window in wonder, Danni hoped the citizens took time to appreciate their city. She was so lost in the new sights and sounds that she didn't notice Bryn staring at her, lost in thought.

They came to the Tiber River, which Danni had studied in college. It divided the city as if flowed north to south. On the east bank lay the classical remains of Rome. She looked at it wistfully as children played happily and splashed each other in the fountain. Blake would have been a mischievous scamp by now if he had lived. She couldn't help but think of him.

"Danni? Danni?" Bryn shook her arm to break her out of her thoughts. "Are you okay? You looked a million miles away."

She smiled at him sadly. "I'm fine. Just tired, I guess."

Bryn wasn't buying it but sensed he shouldn't push her. He hated to see her upset. A smile from her was always like a gift to him.

Ari had hinted that he and Annuska were pondering buying a famous couture house in Rome and joining it with their operation in New York. If they managed to pull it off, it would be the biggest fashion coup to date.

They all stayed at the lovely Hotel da Piazza Venezia. It was an old palace, which had been abandoned after the war and was now a stately hotel, serving the most important guests in the world. And Ari's group certainly was among that special, privileged ranking. He had reserved an entire floor for them.

Danni's room was beside Bryn's. Everything was draped in heavy velvet and silk. A canopied four-poster bed looked so inviting to Danni as the bellhop delivered her enormous set of Louis Vuitton luggage that she hurriedly tipped him so she could jump on the bed to test its softness. She really wanted to take a nap.

But Danni knew that she didn't have time for a nap, so she looked longingly at the bed and mentally prepared herself for what was next. She changed and joined her group for dinner, where they met Constantina da Corso, the outrageous owner of The House of Corso, which Ari and Annuska were desperately trying to get their hands on.

Ari and Annuska's team members spent the evening charming and chatting up the widowed, red-headed, flamboyant woman. Constantina was a unique character who had run the couture house since her husband's untimely demise. He had died in a water skiing accident off the coast of Monaco three years before. He had left his ideas so well-planned that even a monkey could have run things. However, Constantina was bored and wanted to do other things, so the time was right for the Zambinis to make their move.

After dinner, Constantina suggested that Ari and Annuska go back to The House of Corso to talk business, and Ari and Annuska were visibly pleased. On the way out the door of the restaurant, Ari gave his team the thumbs-up behind Constantina's back.

Danni and Bryn were both wired from the wild dinner and decided to check out the city together. They walked through the streets and enjoyed some of the sights. Even at night, it was splendid.

Danni shivered slightly, and Bryn noticed. Ever the gentleman, he slipped his jacket around her shoulders, and she smiled at him. Even though the summer temperature averaged in the seventies by day, it often was much, much cooler at night. Although very becoming, Danni's white silk, halter-style dress with the slit up the front did little to actually keep her warm.

"So, I take it you like the city," Bryn said.

"I absolutely love it," Danni said as they continued to stroll.

Bryn made her feel safe. She had told him about Jeff and Blake and her family not long after they had begun getting to know each other. Danni usually kept that part of her life to herself, but Bryn made her want to let down her guard. He had made it so easy. Ari and Annuska knew about Danni's past too, but Danni decided no one else needed to know. She was keeping her circle tight. Trust was a hard thing for her.

They stopped and looked over the stone bridge into the lapping waves of the Tiber River. Bryn looked like he wanted to say something to her but never did, so she just let it go.

The next day at breakfast, Ari and Annuska announced that they had indeed acquired the House of Corso. Everyone cheered and hugged. It was a great way to start the day. The Zambinis had been granted permission to use some of the castles around Rome for their photoshoots.

First up was the Castle Sant'Angelo. It made a breathtaking background for the shoot. Danni wore a huge fur coat with a leather bathing suit underneath. Thankfully it wasn't risqué. Danni flatly refused to wear anything inappropriate. Ari and Annuska would never have asked her to, anyway. "Risqué" wasn't their style of clothing. Bryn looked fantastic in a new style of tuxedo. The modern clothing was in stark contrast to their historic surroundings, but somehow it all worked flawlessly. And that was part of the magic of the Zambinis.

Danni and Bryn completely owned the shoot from start to finish. What was captured on film was nothing short of magic. They oozed style and class, and the camera loved them both.

Other shoots in unusual wardrobes were held over the next two weeks. They shot at the Villa Farnesia, the Villa Borghese, the Palazzo Corsini, and the Palazzo Doria. Danni was breathless as she surveyed the scenery at night and fell even more in love with the city.

At the end of their two weeks in Rome, the group traveled to Milan, the capital of the Lombardy region of Italy, in the Po River Valley. Danni also loved Milan. It was truly the fashion capital and was much more contemporary-looking to her. She and Bryn found time to visit some of the art galleries there. They even saw Leonardo da Vinci's The Last Supper, housed in the Church of Santa Maria dell Grazie.

But their time in Milan was mostly work. Ari's models were joined by four additional models, who flew in just for this part of the shoot. They helped debut his new line, the one they had been practically living for over the last several months.

As she strode down the runway, Danni felt butterflies. Her long, coltish legs carried her with the greatest of ease. Ari's line was the favorite of almost everyone. He had chosen to use bold new colors and textures. Danni owned the runway. Ari had known it when they bumped into each other in Charlotte, and she had never made him doubt it for a moment.

Constantina's line was fabulous but just didn't have the splash and impact of the House of Zambini. But putting her house together with Ari and Annuska's was going to be pure magic, and they all knew it.

And Danni was the queen of it all. She had arrived. The international papers picked it up, and her photograph was spread all over the world, something she would never have dreamed.

Jana and LaMika were thrilled. They got together back in Charlotte and celebrated and toasted their dear friend. She needed some joy in her life after so much heartache. Everyone was happy for her. Everyone except for the Gradens. Iris, especially, was angry. Through narrowed eyes and a haze of cigarette smoke, she cursed as she looked at her daughter's pictures in the paper. No matter what Iris said or did, Danni was happy and landed on her feet, and Iris remained miserable.

But Danni wasn't thinking about Iris now. It had been a long, hard battle, but she was coming alive again and healing. God blessed her and brought her through the storms and trials, and she thanked Him for it. She laughed and danced and celebrated at a huge party thrown jointly by the Zambinis and Constantina, to announce the merging of their two design houses. It was a wonderful time for all.

23

At the end of the party, Ari hugged Bryn and Danni and congratulated them again on a "job very well done." He couldn't have been happier or prouder of them. He also ordered them to take a few days off and come back to New York after a "little well-earned rest." He held up a hand when Danni started to object. He'd already made arrangements to send the jet back for them at the end of the week, saying he couldn't have his best models looking tired.

And with that, everyone was gone but Bryn and Danni. They giggled like two little kids after deciding to sleep in the next day and then go sightseeing. "Bryn, I've got the best idea ever," Danni said with big eyes and a huge grin over breakfast.

"Lord help us," he said as he helped himself to a banana.

Danni stuck out her tongue. "No, really. This is a brilliant-beyond-brilliant idea."

"Okay, let's have it," he said.

"Let's go to the Mali Coast," she said. She whipped out some pamphlets from the front desk and started telling him her idea.

"Okay, I have to admit it does sound like fun," he said.

"Can we do it? Please?" Danni leaned in and grinned at him. She moved back just a bit when a shadow passed over his face.

"Sure, sure we can," he said.

Danni wanted to ask him what was wrong but was afraid to.

Bryn suggested they get their things together and meet downstairs in half an hour.

"Good, because I've already rented a car for us," Danni said with a wink and disappeared upstairs, way ahead of Bryn.

Thirty-five minutes later, they were crammed tightly into a tiny little car that Bryn likened to a "clown car," making Danni laugh. "Two tall models with all of the beauty products we have need a huge car, not this," he said.

Danni had to agree. "Well, it was all I could get on short notice," she quipped and took off.

Bryn didn't realize Danni had a need for speed, so he hung onto the door handle for dear life as she navigated the many twists and turns on the scenic drive on the coastal road. The view was absolutely breathtaking. There were jagged cliffs and blossoming flowers.

They stopped at a charming seaside village and found two rooms available at the Hotel Santa Caterina. It had a winding garden path the led to the beach. It was perfect. They had five days to relax and swim and not have to worry about anything. They both needed that time far more than either of them could have ever realized.

The second night there, they parted company after swimming and sunning themselves for most of the day, so they could get ready and meet for a bite to eat. Someone had suggested a seafood restaurant within a short walking distance to the hotel, so they were going to try that. Danni came down to meet Bryn in a purple dress that took his breath away. It wasn't so much the dress, although Ari had outdone himself on the design; it was the stunning woman wearing it.

And, if she were being completely honest, Danni thought Bryn was incredible. He was, in so many ways, her best friend. She just couldn't understand why he pulled back from her without warning sometimes. Bryn was such a joy to be around that Danni didn't want to force him to talk to her if he wasn't ready. He was too special to her.

After dinner, they took a stroll on the beach. It was a beautiful night. The stars were twinkling, music was drifting down to the beach from somewhere nearby, and nobody else was in sight. Danni accidentally tripped, and Bryn caught her. Everything stopped at that moment. They stared at each other, and he just kept holding her. Without thinking, Bryn pulled Danni close and kissed her, something he had wanted to do for a very long time.

Danni realized that she had wanted Bryn to kiss her for a long time too. She kissed him back. They stood that way for quite a while, and then just as suddenly, Bryn pulled away from her. "Danni, I'm sorry. I shouldn't have done that. It was a mistake." He nearly stumbled backward.

"Why, Bryn? Why was it a mistake?" Danni noticed the tears in her own voice. "What did I do wrong? I don't understand."

That was Bryn's undoing. He never wanted to hurt Danni. "No, Danni, you didn't do anything. I'm so sorry. I guess it's time I told you," he said with tears in his eyes. He took her hand and led her to a nearby rock, where they both sat down.

"Bryn, what is it? You can tell me anything, "Danni said, concerned.

He sighed heavily. "Danni, I want you to know that I love you."

"I love you too," she said.

"I mean I really love you," he said, looking into her eyes and holding her hand.

Tears slid down Danni's cheeks, but she said nothing more.

"If things were different, I would want to marry you in a heartbeat. We would have a houseful of the cutest babies in the world—thanks to you—and Ari and Annuska would drive themselves crazy outfitting all of us properly."

Danni had to smile at the image he painted. "Why can't we have that? It sounds perfect to me."

"It sounds perfect to me too," Bryn answered. "Danni, you are a rare treasure in this world, especially our crazy world. You're a Christian, a true believer, just like me. You live out your faith, and that is what I love most about you. You are real. Sure, you're gorgeous, which I also appreciate, but I know your heart and I love what's in it. That's what matters most to me."

"I still don't see the problem," Danni said, sniffing.

"Before I ever met you, I was on a shoot on a remote island in the South Pacific. I don't even think it's on many maps, but it makes a great backdrop for a photo shoot. Everything went great until the next-to-the-last day of the shoot. The photographer was really nuts. He was rushing everyone because a storm system was blowing in. He was trying to beat the clock. Long story short, I got knocked off a ladder, and my femoral artery got cut. The island was so small they had to fly me to another island for treatment. It was really primitive conditions. I lost a lot of blood and required a transfusion. Unfortunately, the blood they gave me was tainted." He blew out a breath and hung his head.

"What do you mean 'tained'?" Danni asked.

"I mean, I got AIDS from the transfusion," he said sadly.

"Oh no, Bryn, " Danni was crying openly now, as was Bryn. They wrapped their arms around each other and cried together for the unfairness of it all.

"What can we do?" Danni asked.

"We?" Bryn asked after a while.

"Yes, you doofus, I said, 'we.'"

Bryn smiled and hugged Danni. "See, you are the perfect woman, Danni. But I refuse to marry you knowing I am going to die."

Danni stood up and planted her hands on her hips. "Now you see here, buddy. I understand just how short life is. I've learned that lesson all too well, several times over. If you are blessed enough to find somebody who loves Jesus and loves you, then you need to hold on to that. Period. End of story."

Bryn argued with her. "Danni, I can't put you through that. I won't. I just won't."

"I could die tomorrow in a car accident. I could go on a safari in Africa and an elephant could sit on me and crush me to death. I could get bitten by a snake on a shoot in the desert and die. What about that?" Danni was stamping her foot.

Bryn shook his head sadly. "Danni, I just can't ask you to marry me knowing I am going to die and probably fairly soon."

"Okay, then, fair enough. Then I'll do it," Danni said. She got down on one knee and said, "Bryn Pateau, I love you. So, will you please marry me?"

"Danni, are you sure, absolutely sure?" he stammered, stunned that she would even consider it.

"Absolutely," she replied.

"You are completely nuts. Then, yes, I will marry you, my beautiful lady," he said, pulling her to her feet and kissing her.

They talked long into the night, both of them trying to absorb all that had happened. "Bryn, why aren't you angry? How do you handle it so well?" Danni asked.

Bryn smiled. "Oh, I was angry for a long time—at God, at myself, at the photographer, the doctors who gave me the blood, and the person who donated it. Actually, 'angry' doesn't even begin to name it. I mean, I'm a virgin. I love Jesus, and I've tried to behave myself. I'm certainly far from perfect, but it wasn't like I was careless by the way I was living. I was on a photo shoot and fell off a ladder," he said.

"Then how did it all change for you?" Danni inquired.

Bryn blew out a breath and looked out over the water. The moon was full and bright and literally danced off the waves lapping at the sand before them. "Time. Time and a lot of prayer.

God reminded me that nothing comes to me unless it gets by the throne first. There is a point to all of this, and it's not my place to figure that part of it out. And nobody involved wanted this to happen to me. It was all a stupid accident. It's taught me to really cherish the blessings in my life in a way I probably wouldn't have otherwise." He looked down at her then and pulled her close.

Danni laid her head on his shoulder and hugged him tightly. It wasn't how she dreamed her wedding would all come together, but it all felt right. They prayed together and asked God to bless every day that had together and walked back up the path hand-in-hand.

Bryn and Danni called Ari the next day to tell him the news. He wasn't surprised they had fallen in love. He and Annuska had wondered about it many times. He was a bit surprised that she wanted to marry him, given his diagnosis. They decided to extend their time away by two weeks. They certainly had enough luggage to "tide them over" for a while.

24

Bryn and Danni were married in Italy in an incredibly romantic and intimate ceremony on the beach and spent their honeymoon there. It was tender and beautiful, and everything either of them could have wanted. Bryn was very, very careful with Danni always. He wanted to make sure his diagnosis never became hers. Their one regret was that they couldn't have a child together, but they knew the risk was just too great.

Bryn and Danni even went to Paris to meet his parents, who adored Danni. They cried and hugged her and celebrated the joyful news. They were a sweet, older couple who made Danni feel loved and welcome. She knew, without a doubt, they were some of the sweetest people to ever walk the earth, and it was easy to see why Bryn was so special. It made her sad, once again, to know they couldn't have children, but she refused to dwell on that sadness. Life was too short. Pierre and Marie Pateau were a source of joy for Danni, and she was thankful to know them.

Ari and Annuska threw a lavish party for Danni and Bryn when they returned to New York. The press went wild over the newlyweds, who were all smiles. Danni flew LaMika and Jana up to meet Bryn and attend the party. They loved him and thought Danni made a great decision, and she wholeheartedly agreed.

Still, only Ari and Annuska knew the truth and would have given their lives before they betrayed two people who meant so much to them. They were only sad that Bryn and Danni wouldn't be able to grow old together. But Danni insisted that she would cherish Bryn for as long as they had together, and he felt the same way about her. In rare moments of sadness, Danni always reminded Bryn that an elephant or a snake could get her on a photoshoot, and he always insisted she was incorrigible.

Bryn and Danni decided it made more sense for him to move into her loft. Hers was in a better location and just seemed like a better fit for them. Danni and Bryn made the loft a real home. Bryn was a great cook, thanks to his mom's teaching, and he even taught Danni how to cook. It required a lot of patience on his part, but he was up to the task.

Danni enjoyed being domestic with him. Being married was everything they had prayed and dreamed it would be. They started a Bible study for young married couples through their local church and continued having fun in front of the camera. The key to their success, besides being blessed with great looks, was they didn't take it too seriously. They both enjoyed what they did and had a great time, but they knew it was a blessing the Lord had allowed. They felt that real life was about so much more than what a person wore or how they looked.

Danni pestered Bryn from time to time about having a baby, but he was insistent. He refused to budge and was always extra careful. She was too precious to him to be foolish. She knew he was right, but it still made her sad sometimes.

Danni was always quick to tell people that she had to force Bryn to marry her, and he rolled his eyes at her and laughed. They laughed a lot, danced a lot, and generally enjoyed life. They knew it was precious and fleeting, and they made a decision to move forward and not waste time with regrets. They traveled and modeled and continued to make the Zambinis proud.

About a year after they were married, Bryn and Danni got to

do a shoot together in the Bahamas. Bryn was wearing a new, stylish coat Annuska had designed. Although it was hot, he was well bundled up and completed the look with dark sunglasses. Danni proudly thought he had never looked healthier or more handsome. He worked the shoot like the pro he was.

After a time, the photographer told him to unbutton the coat. When he did, everyone was shocked into silence when he pulled it open to reveal he was wearing a neon green swimsuit with red Santa Clauses all over it. They had to shut down production for ten minutes so everyone could compose themselves again. Bryn just shrugged and blew Danni a kiss. She laughed so hard she cried, messed up her perfectly applied makeup, and Michael and Lauren had to rush in and fix it.

Danni and Bryn celebrated their second wedding anniversary in Italy. Danni said it was extra special to go back to "where it all began."

It was about a month after their second wedding anniversary when Bryn got really sick. It started with the flu, and it spiraled downward from there. Danni and Bryn weren't surprised. They knew it would happen; they just didn't know when. A trip to the doctor and some painful tests confirmed their worst fears.

When Danni realized it was happening, she locked herself in the bathroom, turned on the shower, crawled into the corner, and sobbed into a towel. She loved him. He was a wonderful husband, and she knew she was going to have to say goodbye to him.

That night, Bryn asked her, "Are you sorry you married me?"

"Not even for a second," she said, taking his hand. "We've had more love and laughter and happy memories than a lot of people have in fifty years. There's nothing to be sorry about," she said, hugging him.

Danni called Ari and Annuska after Bryn was asleep. She explained the situation, and they sadly had to plan for such a situation. Ari and Annuska were quietly flying Bryn and Danni to Paris, where they would be met by his parents. They would stay there and keep him comfortable until the end. He would be surrounded by love and out of the eyes of the press.

That is exactly what they did. Bryn lingered for two months, and Danni never left his side. He died in her arms. His last words were, "Je t'aime, beaucoup."

Danni had replied, "Moi, aussi. Toujours."

Bryn was buried on a hill near his parents' farm, and Danni knew she would love him forever. His grave marker read simply, "Bryn Eduoard Pateau, Beloved Husband and Son. A merry heart doeth good like a medicine. Proverbs 22a." It was the perfect tribute to the way Bryn had lived and died. Although he had his share of heartache and pain, he chose to concentrate on the good. His heart was merry, and that was precisely the way he would live on forever in Danni's heart and in her mind.

He had been such a blessing to her. When she felt weak in her faith, he challenged her, encouraged her, and prayed with her. He helped her realize her heart wasn't dead and buried with Jeff and Blake, as she had once thought it was. Bryn had shown her how to live, to really live, again.

Danni felt a little shell-shocked when she got back to New York. This time, she chose not to move somewhere new. Their loft held way too many happy memories for her. Ari and Annuska had made an announcement to the press and just said that Bryn had passed away after a "brief illness."

They kept Danni out of the public eye for a while, which was fine with her. She still wanted to model, but she was also interested in the "behind-the-scenes" action. She loved how Ari and Annuska put colors, textures, and styles together and made it all work. She proved to have quite a talent for it herself, which pleased both Zambinis.

25

Ari and Annuska threw Danni a gala of a party for her twenty-seventh birthday. She was still a raging success in the fashion world. She anonymously donated a lot of money to cancer and AIDS research, continued to run a Bible study, and tried to keep moving forward.

This time, she led a Bible study for widows and other suddenly single women. It was a far cry from the one for young married couples she and Bryn had led, but Danni did her best to embrace this season in her life. She still missed her lost loved ones, but she knew none of them were really lost. Knowing they were all with Jesus and that she would someday join them made it easier to bear.

By this time, LaMika had married a handsome young doctor she had met at the hospital where she worked. They had only dated for a few weeks before deciding to get married. Danni barely had time to catch her breath when LaMika called her with the impending wedding news before she had to catch a plane to Charlotte to attend the wedding.

Danni served as honor attendant and caused quite a stir when she flew to Charlotte for the wedding. The press followed her and nearly attacked her when they left the church to get to the reception. Danni had cried as LaMika exchanged vows with Dr. Benjamin Brantley. They were so happy together, and it made Danni smile to see them together.

Danni wasn't terribly surprised when she got a special phone call a few months later. LaMika was squealing on the other end of the line. She joyously announced that she and Ben were expecting a baby. She called back shortly afterward to correct her statement. They were expecting two babies. Twins!

Danni was thrilled for her friend. LaMika and Ben had two beautiful boys, and Danni was chosen to be the godmother, of course. It didn't hurt to see them like she had feared it would. It helped remind her that God is good, and babies are always a blessing. LaMika and Ben named them Thomas and Travis. They were identical twins, and Danni worried she would not be able to tell them apart.

Danni had been saddened to hear that shortly after LaMika's twins were born, Rachel Kingston died of a heart attack, and Connor had died shortly afterward in a car accident. She suspected that Connor had really died of a broken heart. She grieved for them and thanked God that He had seen fit to place such extraordinary people into her life.

Linda and Daniel Bradley had disappeared from her life, as had Russell. Although it had hurt, she understood there were chapters and seasons in life, and sometimes you just didn't continue in someone's story. She loved them all anyway and prayed for them whenever God brought them to her mind.

Danni also prayed for Andy, who continued to struggle with life. He was serving a long sentence in jail in California. She'd tried to contact him several times, and he refused to communicate with her. She just prayed he would reconnect with Christ and make the most of his life, whatever that turned out to be.

Danni rarely heard from Iris anymore. Once in a while, there would be a nasty phone call from her, or she would send Danni an equally nasty letter, but that was just about it. Ruby had died after a brief battle with breast cancer, and Danni felt almost nothing at all when she received the news from Iris, in a letter sent four months after Ruby's funeral. Danni still had nightmares once in a while, and her stomach troubles were still there, but things were so much better for her now that Danni felt almost guilty dwelling on any of it. But not quite.

Danni kicked off her shoes after a long day and swung her legs up over the edge of the sofa as she settled in to call Jana, who was now Dr. Jana Sharp and happily ensconced at the University of the Carolinas. Literature had always been her passion, and she loved being a professor. They enjoyed a wonderful phone visit, as always.

Jana and LaMika had become close to each other over the years, thanks to Danni, and they all tried to stay in touch with Sharon and Dan, who had finally gotten married. Danni spoke to Sharon and Dan when she could, but her crazy life made it a challenge to stay in touch as much as she wanted to. Danni laughed as Jana told her about LaMika's latest adventure with her boys. They were lively and cute and kept their mommy on her toes, for sure.

After Danni hung up with Jana, she strolled slowly through the apartment, thinking of Bryn. She smiled whenever God brought him to her mind, which was often. It some ways, it seemed like he was just away on a trip, and he would burst through the door any moment with hugs and kisses and silly presents for her.

Whenever he had been around, the air was filled with electricity and excitement. He was always so full of life and had funny stories that made her laugh until she cried. She felt him with her as she looked out at the skyline. It was hard to believe he'd been gone for so long. She sighed sadly as she turned out the lights and went to bed.

The next morning, Danni arrived at Ari's office at nine o'clock for the meeting she had arranged with the Zambinis. She greeted them with hugs and sat down.

"Okay, Danni, what's up?" Annuska asked, leaning in.

Danni took a deep breath and plunged in. She said simply, "It's time I retire from modeling."

"What?" Ari asked, shocked.

Annuska had sensed it coming, but Ari hadn't. She chalked it up to women's intuition, but she had felt it. Danni's work and popularity were as solid as ever, but her heart just wasn't in it anymore, at least not like it used to be.

"Things just aren't the same without Bryn," she said with a small smile. She held up a hand at the sympathetic looks on both of their faces. "Look, I know, I know. But it's time for a new chapter in my life. I absolutely don't want anybody to feel sorry for me. I'm so blessed to have had this time with all of you, and I got to marry my best friend. I got to work with my husband all over the world. That's more than most people get."

Ari and Annuska gave Danni their blessing. She only had another month to fulfill in her contract with The House of Zambini, which gave her enough time to conclude her business in New York.

Four short weeks later, Danni said a tearful farewell to Ari, Annuska, Michael, Lauren, and her favorite fellow models. She was keeping the apartment, at least for now, and would decide later what she wanted to do about it long-term.

She flew to Jamaica for a two-week vacation. She hadn't taken a proper vacation since Bryn died, so she was long overdue for a rest. Danni was looking forward to enjoying two sun-filled weeks on the beautiful island.

Before Danni left New York, Jana had helped her put her plan into motion. Directly after her vacation, Danni was planning to fly to Charlotte to re-enroll at the University of the Carolinas to finally complete her degree. Since she had been forced to give up her scholarship, she would not be eligible for her teaching certificate, which no longer mattered to her. She wanted to finish her degree and write, and she was going to go for it.

But, for now, all was in order, and she was concentrating on relaxing as she sat perched on a stool at an open-air bar and sipped on a ginger ale. The problem was she was spotted about forty-five minutes after she landed in Jamaica, and the photographers tried to swarm her at the bar.

The bartender felt sorry for her and created a distraction while she made her escape. She caught a ride on the back of a local's moped. He took her to an off-the-beaten path hair salon and dropped her off.

Danni told the stylist to "go wild" and he did. He lopped off about ten inches of her hair, which was almost waist-length again. He dyed it a golden brown, which was a lovely change from her original strawberry blond color. It suited her well, and when she left the salon, Danni looked very hip and chic but quite different from her supermodel days. And that was precisely what she wanted.

The next day Danni was enjoying another ginger ale at the same open-air bar where the bartender had rescued her from the press. A television announcer was talking about how Ari and Annuska Zambini shocked the modeling world with news of Danielle Graden Pateau's retirement. A different bartender looked at Danni's photo on television and then looked at her over the glass he was drying. "You dat girl's cousin or somethin', mon?" he asked in an accent that reminded Danni so much of LaMika that it made her smile.

"Nah," Danni replied and shook her head. She smiled and went back to her drink. The bartender smiled and whistled a happy tune as the beach breeze blew a familiar salty wind into the bar. Danni enjoyed watching the sunset over the calm water. She sighed as the blazing sun was swallowed up by the tranquil blue-green water on the horizon.

All too soon, her vacation ended, and it was time to leave. Danni flew to Charlotte. She had made arrangements to stay at a hotel while she looked for an apartment. She wanted to find someplace fun.

On the long-awaited day of Danni's return, Jana had taken the afternoon off, canceling her classes, which was something she almost never did. She met Danni at the gate, and they squealed as they hugged each other like two little school girls.

"You look great, Danni! I love your new look. How do you get more beautiful each year?" Jana asked,

Danni rolled her eyes. "Girl, first thing on the list is to get you a pair of glasses. But thank you. And you look wonderful," Danni said with a smile as she hugged her dear friend again.

They laughed and chatted as they made their way to the baggage claim, where it took Danni, Jana, and two young men they found to help get all of Danni's luggage and presents she'd brought to Jana's station wagon. Jana was embarrassed to still be driving it after all these years, thinking Danni might not want to ride in it.

Danni exclaimed, "You brought Barney!" Barney was Danni's pet name for Jana's car because Jana had always said it was as old as a dinosaur. Danni had said that Barney was the brother car to Jana's parents' car, the one they'd used to move Jana to college when Danni and Jana had first met.

"You will never change," Jana said, relieved, and they both enjoyed a good laugh.

They chatted and made plans all the way to Danni's hotel. After Danni got settled with Jana's help, they went to a trendy restaurant for a bite to eat. It didn't take long for it to seem like the good old days for both Jana and Danni.

Danni was also happy that Jana had made a commitment to Jesus. She could see the peace in Jana's eyes that had not been there before, and she said as much to her.

"I honestly don't know what took me so long. I guess I was afraid, but after seeing everything you have gone through and how you keep on going, I knew that there had to be more to life that just the here and now. Now everything makes so much more sense," Jana stated.

"Oh, Jana, I can't tell you how happy that makes me and how much I have prayed for just that." Danni was beaming. "But trust me, I'm not much of a worthy example. I fall short all the time."

"But aren't you thankful that God doesn't?" Jana asked.

"More than I can ever say," Danni said, her heart full.

Jana's cell phone rang, and it was the university. One of the professors just down the hall from her had her office flooded when a pipe burst. She needed Jana's help moving files and boxes. Danni offered to go and help, but Jana waved her off.

"You go enjoy LaMika and her crew. I'll catch up with you soon. It's so good to have you back where you belong." Jana hugged her and was off.

Danni took a taxi to LaMika and Ben's house. They knew she was returning to Charlotte, but Danni hadn't told them exactly what day. Ben answered the door and whooped when he saw Danni. He gave her a big bear hug and ran to get LaMika and the boys.

Ben was the perfect match for LaMika, Danni thought. He

was fifteen years older than his wife but was a very distinguished gentleman. He was six feet tall with a light dusting of gray hair at his temples. His dark eyes lit up every time he looked at LaMika, which made Danni very happy to see.

"Aunt Dan-Dan! Aunt Dan-Dan!" Tommy and Travis yelled and launched themselves at her. They wrapped their little arms around her long legs and positively chortled with glee.

"Now don't you two hurt your Aunt Danni," LaMika scolded as she came downstairs.

Ben and LaMika peeled the boys off Danni, then offered her a seat in the living room while the boys played with the wonderful, fun toys Danni had brought them. Their home was a beautiful, two-story one done in a Spanish hacienda style. It had been Ben's "little wedding gift" to LaMika.

Before meeting LaMika, Ben had thought he would remain a bachelor doctor, but when LaMika came storming into his life, everything changed, and he couldn't have been happier. Their shared faith helped make theirs a strong and solid marriage.

The adults enjoyed chatting and getting caught up. Having just finished dinner when Danni arrived, the boys soon wore themselves out. Danni insisted on helping LaMika with their bath time. Ben offered to do dish detail so the ladies could chat as they got Tommy and Travis squeaky clean.

Soon, the exhausted boys were clean, asleep, and the dishes were done and put away. Danni chatted with Ben and LaMika for a short time more, hugged them, and caught a cab back to her hotel. She was so thankful for her wonderful friends.

The next morning, Danni went to the university and bought all of the books she would need. The fall session was beginning in two weeks, and she wanted to make sure everything was ready. She used the two weeks to get herself set up in a cute apartment with three bedrooms. She was going to use one as a guest room and one as an office/study space.

Danni also treated herself to a new car. She chose a red Corvette. Although she could certainly afford it, she didn't splurge too much. But every once in a while, she did. Ari and Annuska had made sure all of their people were well taken care of and that they were aware of what was being done with their money. They didn't want anyone taking advantage of their people and stealing money from them, so Danni learned well to be shrewd with her money and her investments, which she took seriously.

Danni drove over to the university, strategically parked her car in an effort to keep it from getting dinged, and took a leisurely stroll around campus. Memories flooded in as she walked around, but they didn't hurt.

Surprisingly, the memories comforted her, reminding her that her loved ones weren't gone. Thanks to Jesus, she knew she would see them again. Now, it was her time to continue on her mission until God called her home.

As she walked, thunder rumbled in the distance, and dark clouds rolled in. Danni was so deep in thought that she barely noticed the weather until fat raindrops began falling.

Danni threw her head back, opened her arms wide, and laughed as she said, "Thank You, Jesus, for bringing me this far. I can't wait to see what we are going to do next!" Even though life could be a painful mess, sometimes, Danni knew that God was always with her, and that she could trust Him to turn it into something beautiful.

The sequel to *A Beautiful Mess* will be released soon!

Be sure to look for *A Blessed Mess: Answered Prayers,* to follow Danni's journey as she seeks to make her dreams come true while struggling with shocking secrets from her past that threaten her peace, her future, and her life.

About the Author

KRISTY NOEL GILLINDER loves inspiring people through the written word and showing them how we all need Jesus and each other. Happily married to her college sweetheart, Rob, they've been blessed with five children, nine rescue dogs, and currently reside in Texas. Kristy is also a fashion model, doll collector, and adores mermaids.

You can contact her at: KristyNoelGillinder@gmail.com or www.ABeautifullyBlessedMess.com.